The white lab rat, threatened by a weapon that could be triggered via the internet, was to live in Florian Mehnert's art installation for eleven days. The internet world followed the livestream in an uproar. A worldwide shitstorm and numerous death threats followed. The art experiment `11 DAYS´ went around the world. How did the interactive art experiment work? Why was the experiment ended on the seventh day instead of the eleventh? Was the audience itself the lab rat in the end? The German artist Florian Mehnert publishes for the first time what really happened.

`11 DAYS´ gives a frightening insight into a society controlled by aggression and hatred.

Florian Mehnert gained international attention with many art projects. In his art project „Waldprotokolle" (2013), he bugged paths and clearings in forests with microphones as a statement on the NSA affair. In his video installation „Menschentracks" (2014), he showed 42 video sequences of hacked smartphones whose cameras and microphones were activated remotely. His photo series REFUGEE STACKS (2015) in which he stacked African refugees on top of each other was his reaction to the situation of refugee flows and an examination of post-colonialism and migration. With FREEDOM 2.0 (2016/2018) Florian Mehnert realised a participatory art installation in public space that asked about an influence of society on BIG DATA. During the pandemic, he created his globally acclaimed photo project „Social Distance Stacks" in which he photographed, among others, dancers of the Stuttgart Ballet in bubbles (2020/2021). Florian Mehnert deals with social and current political issues. In doing so, he works with an expanded concept of art that often focuses on the participation of the recipients.

munihof

Note:
All names are fictitious, all email addresses and Twitter accounts are fictitious or anonymised. The anonymisation is intended to avoid elevating any conflict to a personal and legal level of dispute and thus reducing it.

Bibliographic information of the German National Library: The German National Library lists this publication in the German National Bibliography; detailed bibliographic data are available on the Internet at dnb.dnb.de.

Unabridged edition
March 2023
1st edition 2023
Publisher: munihof © 2023 Florian Mehnert
Cover design: Florian Mehnert
Photography: Installation 11 DAYS, Florian Mehnert
Production and publishing: BoD - Books on Demand, Norderstedt
ISBN: 978-3-75049-4-503

Florian Mehnert

The Art Experiment
11 DAYS
Work Biography

„After the twelfth day, the gun will be pointed at you! No matter where you are: in the mall, in the shop around the corner or on the street. You know a life is worth nothing, then it shall be the same for you."

1...r+4........4@guerrillamail.com

Alexander G.

A young man.
Dark straight short hair. Wide mouth. Dark eyes. Perhaps with severe visual impairment judging by his thick glasses.
His head is slightly lowered. His closed mouth suggests a kind of smile. I only see his photo, which shows him on his Facebook account.
His name is Alexander G. He is interested in the music of the „Böhsen Onkelz"and the „Toten Hosen". Under the heading television he likes the programme `Animals looking for a home´.
Under the category other he links: News from the Smurf, Otto Waalkes, Europa Park, Singen says NO to the asylum seekers' home, cuddly things for rats & co.
I'm sitting in my kitchen behind the counter at a small wooden table in front of my laptop and scouring the website of a pop radio station for initial reactions. On the radio station's Facebook page, I discover a few entries under a short announcement of my project placed there.
Among them a post by Alexander G.:
„Where can I find this so-called artist, I think he needs a bullet through the head!
What they are up to is really perverse."

I am surprised and feel unintentionally affected by his comment.

I then send an email to the radio station's editorial team asking them to delete the entry from their Facebook page immediately. It was a threat.

The radio station complies with my request.

At that time I had no idea that his entry would be the start of a worldwide shitstorm against me.

Friday

It is 9.23 a.m., 13 March.

Two days earlier I confronted the public with my art experiment `11 DAYS´.

My art experiment consists of a milky white plastic box made of one centimetre thick polyethylene, one metre sixty in length and eighty centimetres in height and width. I had the box made by a plastic fabricator.

The plastic box rests on a table-like steel frame with four legs that I welded. A small aluminium turret is screwed to an outrigger on the steel frame, on which in turn a gun is mounted. It is a movable construction built by myself, driven by servo motors and gears, controlled by software scripts via a small computer.

The special thing is that the weapon can be controlled and triggered via the internet. I have attached a webcam to the barrel of the weapon which sends its livestream from inside the box to the world via the project's website. I order the powerful servo motors on the internet. The white gears from a gear shop.

They are unexpectedly expensive.

Weeks before, I spend days researching so-called Sentry Gun and Turret constructions, which were developed for military training or even paintball scenarios. I want to design my own construction and am inspired by photos I find on the internet.

For months I have been working on the preparation of the project and together with a programmer who lives in Texas, USA, I have been tinkering with the software for the weapon control.

His name is Brad.

I found Brad through my research on the net. I come across his small website which is not very up to date. It is difficult to find his email address. I discover it hidden in a PDF file in which he presents a kind of professional portrait of himself.

I write Brad an email in which I briefly explain that I want to build a remote-controlled weapon design. It takes weeks before he replies.

He is interested and asks me if I have a budget.

I have to confess that I don't have one.

Nevertheless, he decides to work with me.

I don't know anything about Brad.

I have never seen him.

We've never spoken on the phone.

I've never spoken to him in person.

I don't know what his voice sounds like.

All our communication is limited to emails and a Google Hangout, where we chat and initially exchange pictures of my controllable weapon design. We never talk about anything private.

I see Brad briefly once, over a low-resolution pixelated livestream he is setting up in his office one afternoon for testing purposes.

Brad gives me a friendly wave.

An unassuming, possibly slightly stocky man with dark hair and a checked shirt. Maybe in his early forties. He wears a beard around his mouth and chin. I wouldn't recognise him on the street. Brad is sitting at a computer. In the background I see a messy purpose-built room and Darth Vader as a life-size plastic doll, or maybe it's just a cardboard Darth Vader stand-up.

I know from his website that he is a Star Wars fan. He also writes there that in his opinion the band Rush is the only true band that ever existed. Much later I learn that he is a red wine lover. The video stream is without sound.

I bought a black, plain paintball gun. Along with the accessories necessary to shoot. A small compressed air bottle with pressure hose, a so-called gravitiyloader and ammunition.

As far as the gravity loader is concerned, I decide on an electronic version, an „electronic hopper", which loads bullet after bullet into the gun barrel with an electronically controlled small paddle.

I have never dealt with a paintball gun before and take a long time to get advice from a saleswoman called Kathy on the phone of an online shop. She speaks German with an American accent.

Kathy is amused by my inexperienced amateurish questions, obviously. She begins to answer my questions in a strangely irritatingly intimate way, murmuring into the phone that she is a „Woodland Gamer":

„How cool it would all feel playing, how painful it would be, especially afterwards..."

A mood of wickedness flows through me. Commanded by her intimate phone voice, I click my weapon items into the shopping cart.

I can call her again any time, she breathes in farewell:

„All you have to do is ask for Kathy."

On the internet, I find photos in paintball forums showing impressive bruises from being shot with paintball guns.

Late at night, I set up a kind of test station in my studio. My turret construction is essentially two perforated aluminium plates bolted together, with carefully integrated servo motors and gears. I attach the turret construction to a threaded rod that I put through a large heavy piece of square steel tubing.

In the meantime, Brad has programmed the software to such an extent that I can initially control my weapon construction locally via a laptop with manual inputs of the angle of movement. In the silence of my studio, the quiet futuristic whirring of the servo motors reminds me of the cold movements of a robot in a science fiction film.

I attach thick drawing paper and cardboard to the wall of my studio, align my gun design with it and fire for the first time with the click of a mouse.

I wince as the dry short bang of the air gun, shatters the silence. The gun, operated with 200 bar air pressure, is louder than I expected.

The paint balls pierce the cardboard and leave a hole in it. The white wall behind it is smeared with yellow-green paint.

I am surprised by the penetrating power.

I realise that it could easily kill a smaller animal and imagine colourful paint balls bursting on a fluffy furry body from a short distance. I then fire several times at an aluminium plate that I lean against the cardboard. The yellow-green paint splashes metres into the surroundings and then flows viscously down the shiny grey surface.

It occurs to me to use red paint ammunition. As my research reveals, there seems to be no red ammunition in the paintball world because of the risk of confusion with blood.

There are paintballs in many colours, but not filled with red paint. After a persistent search, however, I do discover an Australian company that produces blood-red ammunition.

The company calls itself Killerpaintballs and advertises itself as „Zombie Premier" or „Bezerk". The red coloured ammunition is called „Psycho Blood". The product description explains in English: „For the hardcore scenario gamer who wants to add more realism to their game."

There is no option to purchase the ammunition on the Australian website itself.

My email to the company remains unanswered.

The website names a sales partner in Poland and in France.

I reach a man in Poland who speaks poor English via the mobile number given.

I have difficulty understanding him. He tells me that the ammunition is very hard to get and that he doesn't have any. I try my luck at a paintball shop in Toulouse.

No one there can be reached.

My e-mail was not answered.

Days later, I finally reach a man via a mobile number that I have previously noted down from an answering machine in the shop via a sonorous French voice. I explain to him in French my request for blood-red ammunition, repeating several times mimicking a French English accent:

„Killller" and „Psychooo Blood!"

He understands and listlessly explains that he still has some ammunition somewhere.

The man is not particularly motivated.

I insist and ask him to take a look.

I wait impatiently by the phone while he looks and actually finds two boxes.

Days later, I receive an expensive package from Toulouse containing „Psycho Blood". The packaging shows a blood-covered, snarling, grimacing zombie horror face. The white, pupil-less eyes, narrowed to slits, stare viciously at me.

A white rat is supposed to live in the milky white plastic box of my installation.

It shall remain nameless because it is a lab rat.

Lab rats don't have names.

I have carefully strewn the plastic box with wood shavings and also draped a small branch and a cardboard roll inside. Of course, there is also a bowl with water and food. I glued a small square shelter together from white plastic discs and sawed a semi-circular entrance into it.

Due to the size of the box, the rat will have quite a lot of run. I wonder if it might be too cold for it in my studio.

For days I have been driving around the area, visiting pet shops in order to buy a white rat. It turns out to be more difficult than expected.

Either there are no rats, or all rats are multi-coloured. I try to order a white rat from the pet shop at the local hardware store.

„You can't order a white rat from us," the shop assistant shakes his head, but he can take the trouble to see what's in the upcoming delivery. I should come back next week.

A week later I return to the pet shop.

The salesman from last week is no longer there.

But I am lucky. New rats have arrived.

They are coloured rats, but one is white except for a few very small pale grey spots.

I decide to buy this animal. It is a male rat, already relatively large, intended as snake food.

I also ask for a dead, frozen rat.

So-called frozen food.

It is important to me that the frozen rat is also white and

about the same size. The small dark-haired saleswoman with thick black glasses opens a refrigerator with a glass door and pulls out a plastic box. She opens the lid of the plastic box, in which six rats lie stiffly frozen next to each other.

Like in a tin of sardines.

But there are only coloured rats inside.

I am dissatisfied. She is surprised at my persistence.

„It absolutely has to be a white rat as well, about the same size as the live one," I explain.

The shop assistant looks at me sceptically and reservedly. I try to motivate her, to arouse her interest and spontaneously invent something about a theatre film project, mumbling indistinctly. I want to avoid any possible inference to my actual project.

I continue to receive uncomprehending looks. I notice that the shop assistant's glasses are enlarging her eyes. Determined, I step briskly past her to the fridge, open the glass door myself and pull out one pack after another. Surprised, she tolerates my assault.

I open the plastic tins one after the other and actually find a very similar one by chance and have it wrapped up together with the live rat.

I pay 6.90 Euros for the live white rat, and 5.90 Euros for the dead one.

At home, I put the dead rat with the ice cream in the freezer compartment of my fridge. I have a concept about the frozen rat, but I will never implement it.

I bought the frozen rat for nothing.

Later I will throw it away.

Day 1
Wednesday, 11 March, afternoon

On Wednesday, I put my lab rat into the installation in the late afternoon. It excitedly explores the clinically white box. Shortly afterwards, it discovers the small plastic hut, into which it quickly disappears.

At the front of the box is a large cut-out into which the gun with its long barrel protrudes. I have taped off the opening with a thick black film. It is generously gathered around the gun barrel to ensure that the gun can move freely back and forth.

During dinner I watch the movements of the rat. I am excited about the first livestream of my own installation. I have opened my laptop for this right on the dining table next to my plate and called up the test website. Everything works and tingling excitement flows through me.

I feel a brief moment of satisfaction that my project has finally taken shape.

After a while of not looking at the screen and then glancing at it again, the rat suddenly seems to have disappeared. I rush out of the kitchen across the courtyard into my studio and discover the rat in a fold of the black plastic sheeting. In the short time that had passed, it had already discovered the foil as a weak point and had begun to eat a hole in it. It almost escaped into my studio. I block access to the foil inside the box with an impromptu sawn wooden board. I immediately have to make sure that the rat cannot escape from the installation under any circumstances and start constructing a thin sliding disc made of plastic. After a few failed attempts, I develop a working solution in which the disc can be swivelled back and forth together with the gun. I also protect the webcam with its cable on the gun barrel with black fabric tape. I'm afraid the rat might like to gnaw through the cable.

The livestream and weapon control via the internet are working. Brad has programmed a queue. After logging in, each user has 30 seconds to operate the weapon and is then automatically logged out.

I put myself under time pressure.

After months of preparations, I finally want to start the project. Impatiently, I take photos of the installation the next morning and prepare them for publication.

Days before, I work together with Brad on optimisations for the control of the weapon and the performance of the web server. Until the end, I work on details of the design and functionality. Some friends in Germany and the USA act as testers. Brad and I are asking them for log-ins to the weapon control system, for feedback on performance, and for participation in the online survey on the website.

The survey is positioned just to the right of the livestream: „Take part! Influence the outcome of the project!

Every vote counts!

Should the lab rat stay alive?"

You can answer the question with yes, no or don't care.

I have no intention of giving participants any form of influence on the outcome of the project. But I do want to create the illusion of self-efficacy. I want to create the impression that the outcome of the survey could have an impact on the project.

I am interested in finding out what the audience will say. At the same time, the survey should also influence the recipients and prompt them to ask questions.

The survey will ultimately provide additional information for the recipients.

In the end, more than 16,000 participants will vote:

Yes, the rat should stay alive, say 73.8 %.

No, the rat should die, say 18.5 %.

No matter, say 7.7 %.

On Wednesday evening I decide to go public. Three days later, on Saturday 14 March at 7 p.m., an 11-day countdown will begin, at the end of which I plan to load the gun. Anyone can then fire at and kill the rat via the internet from anywhere in the world.

In the programming and web design, I have placed special emphasis on making the weapon easy to use via a smartphone.

I inform the press in an email with a short text and a photo that shows the rat from the first-person shooter perspective sitting on top of its shelter.

I am forced to turn the entrance of the den around for the photo, because otherwise it would immediately seek refuge inside. Fortunately, the rat climbs onto its lair, which helps me to get a few good photos.

In my press release I write:

„The art experiment `11 DAYS´ explores the consequences of surveillance, the use of remote-controlled armed drones. `11 DAYS´ stages armed drone use and shows it for what it is:

Targeted killing as gamification and consequence of total surveillance. A lab rat is permanently monitored via a live webcam stream.

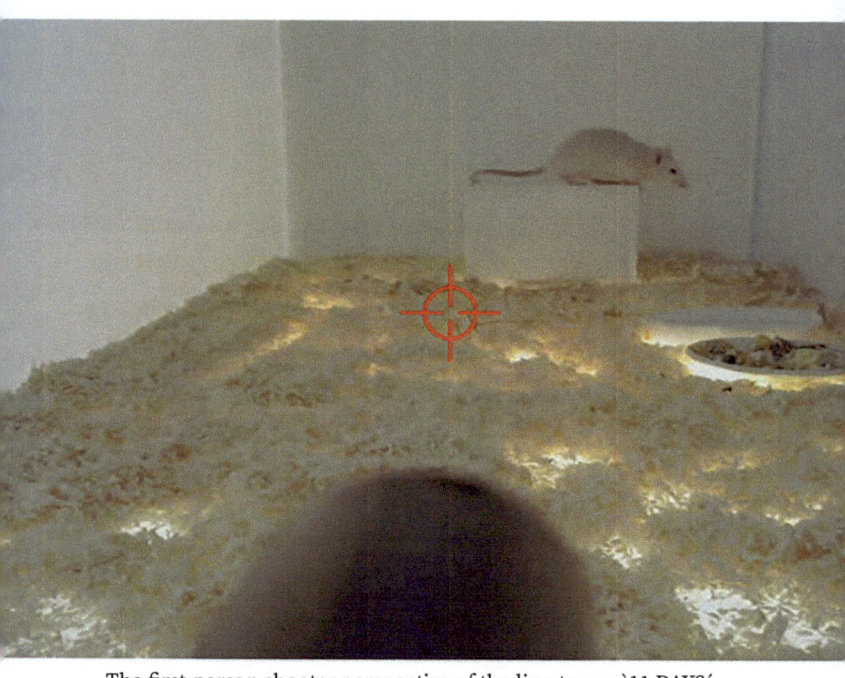

The first-person shooter perspective of the livestream `11 DAYS´

After the countdown of `11 DAYS´ on 25.03.15 at 19.00 (CET), the weapon, which can be controlled via the internet, will be armed. The rat can then be killed from any smartphone, from any computer via the internet.
The countdown starts on Saturday, 14 March, 2015
at 7 p.m. 11days.florianmehnert.de"

I have no certainty about whether my work will find any interest at all. I work for over 6 months towards the moment of publication. Often full of doubts.

This project is preceded by many weeks of conceptualisation, during which I get little sleep. My project arises from my inner need to deal with a problem that is weighing me down. For which I myself see no solution.

I want to draw attention to a consequence of surveillance. I want to show people drastically what effects surveillance has. I want to show what new forms of remote-controlled warfare are being developed with the help of drones. I want to initiate a social discourse on whether new remote-controlled forms of war lead to a possibly greater alienation and lowering of inhibitions. To new gamified sterile brutality that leads warfare into a new dimension of inhumanity. I hope that my project will create a new impulse for discussion, debate and democratic participation. I am dealing with reports about remote-controlled drones executing people in Afghanistan and Waziristan. I am researching intensively and looking for a way of transmission. I want to lure people out of their passivity and indifference, want to make them an integral part of my project. I want to catapult them out of their harmless, comfortable position and make them think. In one of the sleepless nights, the idea of working with a threatened rat arises and I jot down in quick hasty writing:

„Have the audience threaten and kill a rat?"

It is the beginning of the project `11 DAYS´, which at this point has no name.

My installation `11 DAYS´ is lit from below around the clock, which creates a scientific-looking sterile laboratory atmosphere inside the box. I feel sorry for the rat because of the constant lighting, but I don't see any other solution that does justice to a laboratory atmosphere. After all, the video stream from the box has to be visible at night. The rat sleeps in its box during the day anyway and is active mainly at night. Maybe the lighting doesn't bother it as much as I think.

On Wednesday, at 11.25 p.m., two hours after my e-mail announcing the art experiment `11 DAYS´, I receive the first interview request from a major daily newspaper. We arrange a telephone appointment for Friday morning.

Day 2
Thursday, 12 March, 8.24 a.m.

On Thursday morning, I am asked again by the newspaper if it would be possible to do the interview right away.

I boil water and prepare a teapot of Darjeeling while concentrating on my key statements. In my mind I go through them again.

I am very excited and looking forward to the interview. It will be my first interview about the new project. I talk to the journalist on the phone for over an hour.

I have a habit of walking around the house during phone conversations, going up and down the floors. Towards the end of our conversation, the journalist asks if I think someone will end up shooting the rat.

I answer: „Even if you can distinguish between fiction and reality on an abstract cognitive level, the subconscious doesn't separate it. Everything becomes a game. I'm sure there will be some who think it's funny to shoot the rat.

I expect a massacre."

Day 3
Friday, 13 March

On the Friday of the next morning, the article appears. The headline reads, „I expect a massacre!"[1]

I am a little worried about the headline, but reassure myself that it is helpful in drawing attention to my project.

The article is good and correctly portrays the intention of my project.

A few minutes later, the first comments appear on Twitter: „This is not radical, but cowardly and cruel, @FlorianMehnert! (Why not your foot as a target?) …"

Someone asks me by email to cancel the heinous project: „I would like to write to you so that you do not do this heinous ,project' and please cancel it. This project has exactly nothing in common with drone surveillance. I think what you are doing is very bad. You are encouraging people to kill animals and this is simply going too far. You as an „artist" should actually have more in mind.

Since I know that I cannot convince you, I will see what I can do. I hope that this „shitty" project will have consequences for you.

You only encourage people to have even less respect for animals, you encourage people to kill. No matter if human or animal: MURDER IS MURDER! I put this project on the same level as animal testing. For me you are nothing, an animal abuser and not an artist. You should give some thought to the subject of respect for living beings" and says goodbye with: „No friendly greetings".

In the morning I give an interview to a pop radio station. The presenter is delighted and exclaims, „That's spectacular again, Mr Mehnert."
In the following hours, a flood of press enquiries pours in on me.[2]
While I begin to answer one interview request after another and arrange appointments, more journalists keep calling in the meantime.
In an email, a woman offers to take over the rat at the end of the project, as she does not expect me to release it for shooting. She also leaves her telephone number.
Around 12.30 p.m., the livestream breaks down for the first time due to too many requests.
The website is no longer accessible.
The web server, which I rented especially for the project, already seems completely overloaded.
In addition to the interviews I spontaneously give on the phone, I try to find a solution with the provider's hotline.
The solution is to rent a more powerful web server.
More emails arrive.
Somebody says: „The rat should live :`(„.
Another begins with:
 „Dear Mr Mehnert, what is this about?"
and ends with the words
 „without regards".

I don't get to read any more emails and mostly just skim them. The interview requests hardly leave me any time.

Many recipients suggest I should get in the box myself, they wouldn't hesitate to pull the trigger.

Only after hours in the late afternoon can I reach Brad via Google Hangout Chat.

The time difference to Texas is 9 hours.

I describe the server problems to him. He is happy about the unexpected response and starts to look into the stability of the website and the livestream.

I sign a new, more expensive contract with the provider.

The recipients begin to focus strongly on the rat and I try to counteract this in the interviews.

In the process, I keep explaining the role of the rat:

„The lab rat is an important, calculated part of the installation. It is implicitly given the role of the innocent victim and functions as a trigger for attention and emotions. The aim of the project is to initiate a controversial discussion about the consequences of surveillance and the use of armed drones."

The identification of the recipients with the rat succeeds in drawing attention to the project.

I assume that everyone can understand the clear structure and the intended functioning of the installation.

In its construction, `11 DAYS´ creates a parallel situation to the reality of drone wars and first-person shooter games.

What seems shocking is that the installation is fully functional and that one can actually operate and control the weapon via the internet. The website is increasingly critically overloaded as requests continue to rise, so early Friday evening I hire an even more powerful cloud server. I am worried about the now significantly increased server costs, but this is the only way I can maintain the website with the livestream.

Even the powerful cloud server usually runs at its limit for the next few days, but I don't have the means to buy even more power and run several parallel servers at the same time.

Often, more than 200 users are logged into the queue at the same time, each taking control of the weapon at 30-second intervals.

On Friday afternoon at around 2 p.m., two uniformed patrolmen appear unexpectedly in my courtyard. I am on the phone with a newspaper and discover them by chance through the glass door of my kitchen. Worried, I interrupt my conversation while at the same time opening the door with the words: „I'm sorry, I have to hang up, the police are at my door right now".

The two policemen have entered unnoticed through the steel-grey garden gate. They stand in my courtyard and look around searchingly. A brown-haired young man and a young blond woman. Both are duly armed. They are wearing casual dark police jackets, but no caps. I open the door and walk towards them.

They ask me my name.

The policeman has papers in his hand, but he does not show them to me. I don't ask for them either.

The two officers seem cautious and suspicious.

The policewoman examines me closely.

She asks the questions, the man stays in the background.

The policewoman formally tells me that they have been ordered to check what is going on here.

She stiffly lists what she knows about my project and asks me if the facts are correct. I answer in the affirmative.

They know that I claim to be threatening a rat with a firearm and they would like to see the rat and the gun.

They obviously don't have a search warrant with them, but I act friendly and courteous. I approach the policemen and ask them to accompany me to my studio.

I think I sense that my openness makes them rather more suspicious.

They follow me and I feel their tension at my back. Perhaps they think I am unpredictable or crazy. In the studio, I show them the installation and begin to explain my project in detail. Out of the corner of my eye I notice the policeman looking around cautiously.

I wonder if he finds the sight of my converted barn disconcerting. Perhaps he is also looking for possible other extras. Both seem to find my installation curious and bizarre. During my explanation of the content, the blonde woman with accurately made-up eyes seeks constant eye contact with me. She literally pierces me, as if in this way she could look inside me and be certain about the truth of my statement. I am irritated and cut my statement short while I hold her gaze and stare back abruptly. The situation between us seems staged, acted out.

Attentively and intently she follows my every move. I assume that she must have learned this in her training as a policewoman. I take up my explanation again in an emphatically casual manner.

However, she doesn't seem to follow me in substance.

The man stands offset near the entrance door, probably with the intention of securing the situation from the background if necessary. I get the impression that she is not at all interested in the explanations of my artistic concept, which I explain in a motivated, lively gesticulation.

A feeling of embarrassingly caught naivety spreads through me. At this point, the local police already know much more about the reactions to my project than I suspect. Only later do I learn that in the meantime numerous complaints have been received all over Germany and that the investigations of the public prosecutors have therefore already begun. There is also an enquiry from the State Criminal Police Office on her desk.

Hesitantly I realise that the two policemen have of course only come to do their job.

They are to assess whether I am dangerous and, above all, to check the weapon. They have undoubtedly not come to listen to my artistic intention.

I willingly show them the rat in the box and the gun mounted outside. The policeman recognises the paintball gun with a trained eye and is relieved. Shortly afterwards, the two police officers leave my studio without further explanation.

As they close the garden gate behind them, I return to my installation and observe the rapid jerky movements of the gun. The rat has crawled into its lair, only its snout peeking out in a sniff. I listen to the whirring of the electric motors. Without interruption, the users line up in the queue by logging in. They enter the silent, gliding process of waiting for their turn to finally take control of the weapon. The trigger of the weapon, which can be moved by a small servo motor, is constantly being pulled.

Sig-sig', sig-sig', sig-sig'.

The sound is pleasant, gentle.

It only takes a determined click of the mouse or a quick tap on the smartphone to trigger the gun.

It is important for me to draw attention to the aspect of gamification.

Gamification as a playful element in a non-game context.

Playful killing.

We humans have known this for thousands of years.

As children, as adults.

Inflicted death as a powerful experience of superiority, out of self-defence, revenge, hatred or curiosity.

From my childhood I know the disappointment, the little shock, the discovery of the fragility of life.

As a six-year-old, I had caught grasshoppers and put them in a jar to watch them. Maybe five or six. For some reason I had put them in the dark cellar. Maybe I didn't want to see them in my room. Maybe I wanted to hide what I had done from the gaze of others.

I was uncomfortable.

I also felt disgust.

Somehow I felt sorry for the locusts, but on the other hand there was also a kind of interested dislike for the insects. When I went to check the next day, half of the grasshoppers were no longer alive. Some of the survivors had lost a leg or their antennae.

Had they been bitten off?

All in all, the grasshoppers were not well.

Their movements were lame and powerless.

Angular they climbed around.

With a suddenly guilty conscience and pity, I released the last survivors outside. Hoping they would live on.

A little later in the summer I tried to burn small red velvet mites on the stone slabs of our terrace through the concentrated focus of a magnifying glass.

We humans like to play.

We like to play all kinds of things. Football, war, peace, destroying and rebuilding.

And we also love to watch others play.

In the `11 DAYS´ installation, you can do both.

You can play and watch others play. The victim is a rat.

How sweet, how mean, how disgusting, the poor rat, it can't help it.

The attraction is in knowing that the weapon works.

The fact that when the countdown ends, you can shoot.

Surely one will pull the trigger!

Or many in a row!

The fact that the firearm can actually be controlled via the internet, tens of thousands will succumb to this fascination again and again during the countdown.

It is tempting to try it out.

How close is the computer game to reality?

How far is the drone pilot, sitting in front of his joystick and screens, piloting a drone to its destination, from the game? Can we really distinguish between this in our subconscious? The game and reality? Where does a clear boundary define itself?

In the first-person shooter game, everything is fiction.

No one dies, it's not people, it just looks that way, it's just animated images. There on the screens in the drone pilot's container, there they are real images, of real people.

And yet they are just video streams flickering on screens. From an aerial perspective, from above, from satellites, from drones, sometimes distorted and abstracted by poor quality. The playfulness lowers the inhibitions, where something looks like a game, you can kill with laughter and pleasure. Where you sit in safety, far away from the game, where you can be spectator and player at the same time. A film so exciting that it can draw us into its plot. It speeds up our heartbeat, makes our palms damp, even though they are only actors and everything in it is fiction.

In which no real blood flows, in which there are no real dead people, even though it looks like there are.

Why do we find that exciting, even though everything is fiction? Young children are often not yet able to distinguish fiction from reality.

For them, fiction, their own fantasy, is just as real as their real surroundings. They are afraid of fantasies. They are afraid of the actions in films.

Children have to believe what they see.

Adults think they know the difference. We believe we can accurately distinguish between fiction and reality.

Can we control our subconscious and are we in control of it all? Will the rat die in the installation? Will the gun be loaded at the end of the eleven-day countdown?

Will someone shoot the rat via a mouse click?

Where do reality and fiction merge?

Do the participants in the `11 DAYS´ project anticipate a reality that may never happen?

Why does the American military acquire soldiers at the big game fairs? Why does even the German Bundeswehr acquire soldiers at the annual Gamescom fair in Cologne? What do computer war games and computer-controlled weapons of war have to do with each other?

I spray silicone into the movable plastic construction where the weapon barrel protrudes into the box of the installation. There, where the plastic plates rub against each other. The silicone significantly reduces friction and is largely odourless.

Visitors give themselves nicknames to log in:
„Hitler"
„Rat Killer"
„Nazifucker"
„cunt"
„savetherat"
„ratkiller"
 „kill the rat,"
„fuck the rat"
„fuck the artist!"

New emails keep arriving, their senders pleading or insulting me.
Amelie writes:
„Please, please, please don't!" Please go within yourself and realise that what you are doing is WRONG..."
Another email from Christine states:

„I have been thinking about your project all day now. About whether the rat will die.

Whether it is naive to believe in any other outcome.

Whether the gun is even loaded.

Whether you (pardon!) are actually full of shit.

Whether it hurt to pick that one rat.

Whether it is actually what art can and should achieve. Whether it's reprehensible that this project affects me more than the fact that people are dying from drones. Whether it is, after all, a beginning to feel bad about it. Whether it's the beginning of the end to think about (possibly) saving the rat by purposefully missing it, or to take aim yourself right away before someone else maims it. Whether one should feel bad about even thinking about watching the end of the countdown. An artist friend once said to me that the only purpose of art is to encourage you to engage with it. If he's right, then you've got it."

Will the fire really be opened on the rat.

Will the rat really die?

Yes, it will die.

Its white fur will be torn open by the red bullets.

It won't be dead right away.

Maybe a shot to the abdomen first.

Blood spurts out, or is it the red colour of the paintball?

Is something squeezing out?

The beautiful pure white box is stained with blood.

Or is that paint?

The litter turns red. The 30 seconds are up.

The rat goes lame and tries to escape.

It's someone else's turn. Aim quickly and fire the three shots allowed. Miss.

Next one's turn... The rat tries to retreat into its den.

But under the continuous fire of the participants, it no longer succeeds. The rat dies, shot anonymously over the internet. Game over!

That is how it will be.

There is no other option.

No other conceivable way out.

We anticipate and define a reality that is inescapable. I can only skim and take cursory note of all the emails that reach me. I have no peace and time to think about their content. I am under concentrated pressure, on the one hand to answer and coordinate the constant interview requests, on the other hand to look after the collapsing web server and the video stream during short breaks. Again and again I have to restart the local or server-side scripts on the computer that controls the installation.

Only many days later do I find the peace to read what all the people have actually written to me.

Arusa81 writes:

„Is your ‚art' no longer enough to be in the limelight?

If you want to make a difference, then do it with your life. Stand in front of your gun just before the countdown and show the world that you are doing everything to make a difference.

The funny thing is that I didn't even know you existed until now. I read about it on the internet.

And many others feel the same way I do.

So the previous statement is true, that you antisocial dumbass want to kill a rat because you don't seem to be able to get anything done with your own performance.

As I said, stand in front of your own gun and do the world a favour.

Every rat in this world is worth more than you will ever be. Fuck You!!!"

At 2.35 p.m., a major tabloid newspaper answers the phone.

I first cautiously express my concerns to the journalist about whether she is willing and able to accurately portray the intention of my project.

We talk about it at length.

She convinces me by saying:

„Believe me, we can do it!"

I trust her and engage in a conversation.

The article then also appears as a truthful interview.

The headline reads:

EXECUTION PLANNED AT THE CLICK OF A MOUSE.

I arrange a live interview with a Berlin radio station for Saturday morning at 9 am.

Then at 10.30 a.m. another interview and in the afternoon an interview with a North German culture station. I choose longer intervals between the agreed interviews so that I have time for the permanent new requests in between. Until the evening I work through the requests by e-mail or on the phone.

Rainer H. writes:

„Hey,

Great project, which addresses a very important topic,

which is hardly noticed in our time. People are more willing to kill in a virtual world than to pick up a gun in real life. The topic is becoming more and more important in times when global war is practically only carried out with a joystick. But one should urgently differentiate between simulation and reality.

I am a pacifist and have been playing video games for 30 years... I've already killed millions of pixels and in real life I don't hurt a fly. For me, the competition is more important than actually pulling the trigger and „killing". First person shooters have become less and less important to me over the last 30 years. Currently, I prefer to play so-called MOBAs such as Diablo3, DotA2 or LoL (although you also have to kill a lot of pixels there). It only becomes dangerous when the clearly defined boundaries become blurred and you no longer perceive reality.

The whole thing is seen as a simulation, e.g. killing real people on the computer with a drone, and the whole thing is seen as a video game. This lowers the tolerance threshold and also the sense of guilt. That is the real dilemma.

Where does the simulation end and reality begin?

The Milgram experiment is also very interesting in this regard. I will definitely follow the project with excitement, even though I already know that the rat will survive in the end :)

However, there will undoubtedly be a lot of people who will pull the trigger without any scruples (I am not one of them). The reason for this is lack of empathy and a pathological / faulty view / perception (psychopaths).

Kind regards R.H."

At 11.04 p.m. a major newspaper makes an urgent photo request. I send a photo of the installation and the rat in the crosshairs.

At 1.25 a.m. Jens T. writes:
„How about instead of abusing a helpless creature, you put your head in front of the shotgun? Why don't you just swap with the rat?!?!
I'm sure someone will be found to cure you of your moronic ideas... In the „service of your perverted science", of course, with a headshot;-)
Respectfully, Jens T."

The hits continue to rise. The video stream keeps breaking down. There are usually around a hundred players logged into the gun controller:
„Wayne"
„Ratkiller"
„Bang"
The server collapses around 1.50am.
Brad takes care of the reboot.
I sit with my laptop next to the installation until 3am on Saturday, working with Brad to stabilise the server's software and the gun's functionality.
We decide to move to a more powerful cloud server for the next day. I sleep badly and shallowly.
I can't switch off.
At 5.54 a.m. Tatjana L. writes.
„Your rat experiment is not art, it is pure sadism. This is

no way to treat living beings. First you torture them and then you execute them. It doesn't matter at all whether it is „only" a rat in your eyes. Shame on you. Break it off ..."

Day 4
Saturday, 14 March

A Swiss tabloid knows at 6:34 a.m.:

„German Florian Mehnert is having a rat shot for an art project. Anyone can take part. The artist is now being bombarded with protest emails."

My day starts at 6:55 a.m. with the Twitter message:

„Honest would be Florian Mehnert putting himself in the box. Yes, with launch."

XbXXr9X tells me via email:

„You cowardly pig,

why don't you put yourself in the box, you cowardly pig?!
..."

@s[xx]_poy Twitterpost gives me hope:

„Very clever comment on drones; Florian Mehnert set up „installation" so internet users can shoot a rat using their keyboards"

But V...t Girl contradicts:

„@....._@FlorianMehnert MURDERER. I truly hope that if that poor rat gets killed, you do too. You deserve to be shot in the head."

At 8.27 Julian writes from Switzerland:
„After the `11 DAYS´are over, can you also shoot you miserable filthy Nazi with the click of a mouse…?"

At 7.24 @D…K…D…A tweets.
„@FlorianMehnert I hope you get shot one day."

At 8.39 email 1…r+4…….4@guerrillamail.com writes:
„After the twelfth day the gun will be pointed at you! No matter where you are: in the shopping centre, in the shop around the corner or on the street. You know a life is worth nothing to you, then it shall be the same for you."

I repeat myself several times on the radio:
„Tonight on Saturday evening at 7 p.m., the 11-day countdown will begin. Starting today, the rat will live for eleven days. Eleven days that we can use to discuss. To reflect on whether we approve of the consequences of surveillance. Whether we want people to be executed on suspicion with armed drones. Without trial and without a hearing."

According to Guardian statistics, 1147 people were killed in executions by drones of 41 men. For every drone casualty, an average of 28 other people die.[3] Often children as well. After my previous art projects, which mainly deal with the illustration of surveillance (the forest logs[4] and the video installation Menschentracks[5]), I am interested in creating a work in which I can illustrate the consequence of surveillance. It is important to me to give the recipient a decisive participatory role, to put him in a critical situation in which he himself is the monitor and decision-maker.

One drastic consequence of surveillance is the use of remote-controlled armed drones.

A drone operation is preceded by extensive surveillance, based mainly on private data from mobile phones, but also on so-called metadata obtained from the victim's behaviour on the internet. By monitoring and analysing the data, the victim is selected and his whereabouts localised. Those who know the movement profiles of their victim through surveillance know where they will send the deadly drone.

`11 DAYS´ stages the armed drone operation and shows it for what it is: targeted killing as a consequence of total surveillance.

Gamification plays an essential role in this.

The recipient puts himself in the position of the drone pilot. The principle that the installation `11 DAYS´ reflects, and basically emulates in its entire structure, corresponds on the one hand to the control of armed drones and on the other hand to the principle of the first-person shooter video game. In my opinion, the use of gamification leads to a lowering of inhibition thresholds.

`11 DAYS´ refers to the numerous games in which the readiness for aggression and the willingness to kill are staged and initiated.

In the afternoon, I repeatedly discuss the completely overloaded server with Brad.

The statistics show over 60,000 streaming views in a few hours. The server software of the weapon control also seems to be overloaded and can only be kept functional by regular restarts. Time and again, the web server is also hit by DDOS attacks. Obviously, there seems to be someone who is working persistently to bring the web server to its knees again and again.

Sometimes Brad observes the attacks while we are chatting and is able to bring the web server back up shortly afterwards.

British radio asks me for interviews in several emails.

Brad sends me an updated script he has prepared for me. I use it to update the Arduino board on the weapon controller.

Brad often accesses the small computer directly from Texas, which is an integral part of the installation and is responsible for enabling the weapon control via the website and transferring the live stream to the web server.

Seven minutes before the start of the `11 DAYS´ count-down, there are over 200 players in the weapon control at the same time. I load a new script onto the server one minute before seven p.m., which starts the eleven day countdown.

Shortly afterwards, the server is attacked by another DDOS attack. There seems to be really well organised resistance.

Shortly after, Twitter notifies me of a tweet from:

@spr..eb...k

„It's so easy to save the rat.

We just have to want to.“

The server collapses again half an hour later at around 8.17 p.m. under new attacks.

Good thing there's Brad who keeps restarting the server while I try to sleep at night.

A start-up emails me offering to host the server for free in exchange for an advert. I don't have time to deal with the well-intentioned offer. It would take a lot of effort to set up the server there again.

In a lengthy chat, I open up to Brad:

„Brad, I don't know how much longer I can withstand the pressure of all these comments and these idiotic discussions about saving the rat.

After all, my intention of the project is not:

I'm going to kill a rat in eleven days!

I may well abandon the project by the middle of the week."

Brad hardly addresses this, he is too busy stabilising the server.

Meanwhile, the number of people waiting in the weapons controller has increased to over three hundred players.

Day 5
Sunday, 15 March

In the evening at 8.38 p.m., an English newspaper asks for photos of the installation.
In the evening I tweet:
#11days, do you accept targeted killing as gamification and the consequence of total surveillance? this #rat can save 1000's of human #lives

Mdhater replies:
@Mdhater
@FlorianMehnert pathetic attention whore

Day 6
Monday, 16 March

Around 2 a.m. in the night my private landline phone rings. It must have been ringing for a while, because it takes me a while to identify the sound as real from my sleep.

Still drowsy, I think about who could be calling at this hour.

I lie in bed and listen to the ringtone.

It makes me feel eerie.

As it keeps ringing, I decide to look for the phone. I have to go down one floor first and find it lying on a dresser.

As I pick it up, I listen to the static.

I dutifully call out „Hello" a few times into the silence and then hang up. I then switch off the phone and after a while fall into a restless, shallow sleep.

I wake up again at 3.04 a.m. and can no longer calm my thoughts.

I feel lonely and have an urgent need to talk to someone.

Only Brad in Texas might be available at this hour.

I sit down at my laptop and open our shared Google Hangout:

Me: „Brad are you there?"

Brad: „Hey"

Me: „Hey"

Brad: „I was just online making sure the web server was up and running... are you thinking about stopping the project?"

Me: „Yeah, I'm getting too many emails from people wishing me dead, death threats and other forms of aggression"

Brad: „That's crazy, I'm sorry...are you worried?"

Me: „Yes, for my family too".

Brad: „I understand... it's really crazy (and ironic too) that people would do something like that, but of course you can't risk exposing your family to that"

Me: „It's difficult for me to judge how serious all this aggressiveness is. But it's enough if there is only one crush..."

Brad: „Yeah, if you think it could become a problem..."

Me: „The reactions are disproportionate to the reality. The multitude of emails directed at me personally, all the comments on blogs, media and social media show that a lot of people are more incensed about the possible death of the rat than they are about losing their privacy and freedom to total surveillance... especially the aggression against me personally is going to be difficult for me..."

Brad: „I know ... it's stupid ... And ironic ... that they all threaten violence ...do you really think some of them are serious?"

Me: „I don't know Brad ...there are crazed people out there. Islamic terrorists have already murdered cartoonists in Paris.... maybe there are people who are just using the experiment as a platform for their extreme aggression."

Brad: „Well, it's not worth risking your life or your safety... you could write something about the intention of your project, or how successful it is, you can point out all the important aspects... but I don't think you should stop the project because of the reactions or threats."

Me: „No, if I finish the project I will make a statement about it, but you're right, I shouldn't finish the project because of the threats."

Brad: „You could also speed up the project so people can see that in the end the rat won't die."

Me: „Yes, that's an idea. But in terms of all the aggressiveness and countless comments, I don't think it's good to give people real shooting scenarios at the end. It could be misunderstood."

Brad: „Yeah, no shooting ... you should name the rat and have t-shirts printed that say - I saved the rat - haha, ;-) „

Me: „You know, an hour ago the phone rang and when I picked it up no one answered, that was really creepy. We need to plan for the early end of the project, Brad. I don't want to jump the gun tonight ....

Brad: „ugh, yeah"

Me: „but I actually think the project has reached its goal and I should end it promptly."

Brad: „ok"

Me: „Anyway, the discussions won't die down right away... We'll put „game over" in the counterscript (instead of the countdown) at the end. I think we should leave the livestream open and just disable the weapons feature."

Brad: „yeah, good...the animal rights people will see that way that the rat is ok."

Me: „sure, I'll share that it was never intended to open up the possibilities of shooting the rat."

Brad: „People don't realise they are the rat, ‚LOL' :-))..."

Me: „YES!!! LOL, maybe we should just show the empty box and take out the rat as the object of abuse..."

Brad: „Take a nice picture of you and the rat first!"
You could also put up cardboard cutouts and have people shoot them, that would be fun haha..."

Me: „Haha, you mean take a picture of me and the rat to revamp my image, and get people's sympathy back?"

Brad: „Yeah, maybe, LOL...yeah, that could work and we could start the ‚Save the Paper Buddies' campaign, LOL, haha ..."

Me: „Yeah, a lot of the people are curious to see if the gun really works, but like I mentioned, it could be misunderstood by a large portion of the public."

Brad: „well, I'm sure people are very convinced that the gun works"

Me: „yes, definitely"

Brad: „I'm doing some recording of the lifestream right now... the rat is out and active.
I'm uploading it to the server, perfect pictures ...!
I hope we get some good pictures of the end too ..."

Me: „Yes, but as the mood is, we can't let people shoot at the end. I'll think some more about a good, early ending."

Brad: „Good!"

Me: „Brad, thank you very much, you have helped me a lot to calm down a bit and come to the realisation that the early ending has to be well planned"

Brad: „no problem, aah Florian, someone is hitting the server again and trying to crash it..."

Me: „again! :-(„

Brad: „I'll do a reboot".

Me: „Ok, thanks"

„I think I should try to sleep some more,. I still have three hours before I have to go out again ..."

Brad: „Aha, ok, I always have a glass of wine before I go to sleep, haha, look the rat climbs on the gun barrel and looks at the camera ... I recorded it ...the website is pretty slow again right now ....

But, hey, sorry, you need to sleep!"

Me: „Yeah, I think I'm planning on the end of Tuesday or Wednesday".

Brad: „Ok, sounds good"

Me: „so I'm going to jump back in my bed, we'll talk tomorrow ok?"

Brad: „ok, ...goodnight!"

At 8.50 a.m. on Monday morning the provider writes:

„Please check your server for its load and exceeding the set limits. Helpful for this are the outputs of the two shell commands ‚top -bcn 1|head -n 15' and ‚cat /proc/user_beancounters'.

Especially the parameter is exceeded very often.

tcpsndbuf - Total size of buffers for sending data over TCP network connections.

The tcpsndbuf parameter depends on the number of TCP sockets (numtcpsock) and should allow the allocation of a minimum buffer memory for each socket..."

At 9 a.m. I have an interview with a Cologne station at 11.30 a.m. another one with a cultural station.

Then with television.

The TV department of a news agency asks for a filming appointment.

Around 12 p.m., I receive a call from the internet provider. An employee tells me that he has the task of informing me that my cloud server on which the `11 DAYS´ project is running will now be switched off.

When I ask him why, he briefly explains that my project violates the company's terms and conditions and is also immoral.

I insist and shout into the phone that this is not possible and that I do not have the right to simply shut down my server. The employee replies that this is not his decision. It was his job to inform me of this.

I then dial the number of my lawyer friend, who is also immediately available. He promises to do his best to prevent a shutdown. In between other interviews, he calls me back an hour later.

He drew up an affidavit for me to send to the provider by e-mail. He was able to intervene there successfully.

The server then remains online.

A little later, a villager I had never met before appears at my garden gate. He hands me fresh apple juice he has made himself. We speak only briefly. The sympathetic, friendly man expresses his deep respect for my project and wishes me continued strength.

I am very happy about this personal, encouraging gesture. The apple juice tastes refreshing.

I find a postcard in the letterbox.

The card comes from a couple from the village. The front

of the card shows an idyllic motif with cows in the meadow. In the background you can see vineyards in the sun.
„We think your project `11 DAYS´ is good and courageous. The reactions on the Internet are to run away!
Only where?"“

A French TV team arrives at 2.30 p.m.

A reporter from the Swiss cultural radio station has also registered with the team. He arrives around 1 p.m. and stays longer.

I do a reportage-style interview with him while I discuss the shoot with the cameramen.

The Swiss reporter is very sympathetic.

He notices my effort.

I am open and talk about the threats, my worries, about how much the focus is on saving the rat. It is one of the few moments when I find some time for reflection.

A personal, interpersonal conversation develops. I seek the conversation too. I long for an exchange.

Find little opportunity to talk about my thoughts.

Why is there so much focus on the rat?

At times the reactions seem exaggerated to me, some downright insane. Do the people out there really not understand my intention?

Or do they not want to understand the project. Isn't the parallel situation that my installation creates overly obvious? Is it so difficult to realise that the rat functions as a placeholder? As an emotional identification. As a trigger of attention. Everyone can understand the clear structure and functioning of the installation. In its construction, the

`11 DAYS´ project has created a parallel situation to the reality of drone operations.

Is this what touches people so much?

Are they looking for a way out of the hopelessness of reality?

I ask the reporter my questions and he answers:

„With your project, you have hit the issue so hard that some people are simply overwhelmed by it.

Be proud of yourself, you are doing a great job."

I feel no pride. My thoughts are making me sleepless and I am under a lot of pressure.

I shoot with the French camera team in the studio, directly in front of the installation. I speak German with the reporter, my sound is later translated for French television.

In another radio interview I repeatedly explain my intention.

The reporter has come to see me in person for this and we sit facing each other on a sofa with a coffee, occasionally glancing at the inner courtyard.

In the interview, I talk about the culture of targeted killing. Also about the fact that Germany actively supports the use of American armed drones by transmitting video data.

I explain that the `11 DAYS´ experiment is the staging of what drone use actually is.

I ask the question, „Do we want to accept targeted killing by drones?"

When I listen to the interview later, a spokesperson for the public prosecutor's office then also has his say in it:

„There has not yet been a violation of the Animal Welfare Act. This is only the case when the animal is killed. First of all, the person who shot the animal is responsible. As far as the artist is concerned, incitement to commit a crime must be examined. For this to be the case, however, the artist must have had the intention to kill the rat."

I say in the interview: „The aim of the art project `11 DAYS´ is definitely not to kill a rat. It seems that the outrage over the possible death of a rat is greater than the outrage over the actual killing reality of armed drones."

To the reporter, I let slip in the abstract that I may be considering an early end to the project.

The reporter comments later on the radio:

„Maybe the lab rat will win in the end".

„We'll see what happens to the rat in the end," is my original comment, which the reporter cut into the interview as the last sentence.

Early Monday evening around 6.30 p.m.

I decide to go to the local police to apply for personal and property protection.

I scour my emails for threats and death threats and print them out. I can't eat dinner and only drink water and coffee.

The multitude of threats makes me feel unsafe. Every time I walk out of the house to my studio, I feel like I'm being watched and look around on all sides first. The inn opposite would make an excellent observation post.

Some rooms have windows that give a good view of my courtyard.

When it gets dark, I don't like to be near my windows. I fantasise that someone could shoot at me through a window from the street.

I start to suffer from fearful imaginings of someone breaking into my house at night and waking me up standing by my bed with a gun in their hand.

I imagine someone ambushing me sitting in a car. The moment I leave the house and step out onto the street, he starts the engine, howling, and gives it full throttle. The car speeds towards me and tries to kill me.

Many of the threats made to me will not be serious. Some come from England, America or other countries further away. But many also come from German-speaking countries. Is one fanatic enough in the end?

Only one who carries out his threat. Perhaps someone who acts spontaneously, who does not announce it beforehand. Maybe a quiet fanatic who has been following the project and the reactions to it closely from the beginning. Who allows himself to become more and more inflamed by the mood.

Who doesn't give himself the nerve of a threat or who doesn't have the stupidity to warn of his planned action and threaten me.

Perhaps a silencer in whom anger boils up for days, who plans his act in secret. One who vigilantly follows all the agitated or aggressive comments in the social media and does not even participate in them.

One who takes action and doesn't talk away.

One who calmly makes his way to me.

With my printouts in hand, I enter the local police station. I step in front of a kind of bank counter with a thick glass pane and an intercom in a secure anteroom.

No one is there.

I can see the desks, computers and shelves through the glass into the room.

I ring the bell.

A door to an adjoining room opens and two officers enter the large office with the switch-like window where I am standing. A middle-aged man registers me and moves in my direction. Arriving at the counter, he greets me reservedly. I give my name and tell him that I want to apply for personal protection.

He looks at me for a short while and then turns to his work colleague with whom he had entered the room earlier. He walks a few steps away from the counter to his table, where his colleague has taken a seat in the meantime.

He leans close to his colleague. The two seem to be discussing something.

I can't hear what they are talking about because no sound can penetrate the thick, hermetically sealed glass pane.

I observe the conversation between the two officers, which I assume is about who should be responsible for me. The sitting policeman turns his head and looks over at me. Shortly afterwards, he stood up and came to me at the window. He tells me to sit down and please wait.

I sit down opposite the window on one of the chairs against the wall and wait.

A good quarter of an hour passes, during which I have the opportunity to study the small anteroom.

Opposite me are the usual wanted posters on which you can see wanted criminals in black and white photos. I have been familiar with the design of these posters since my childhood, when they were looking for RAF terrorists. The design doesn't seem to have changed all these years.

Often a red, bold font is used. Then it's always the same raster-like sequence of black-and-white faces staring blankly into the camera. The photographs look as if they were taken in the sixties or seventies. The hairstyles and moustaches are not contemporary. I wonder who ever studies these faces, who memorises them so much, or finds them so memorable, that they are able to actually recognise one of these faces somewhere in the supermarket or on the street.

My gaze falls on more posters on which the various police emblems seem more important than the messages themselves.

Preventive protection against burglary in the house or a cycling course for children in road traffic.

The metal chair becomes uncomfortable.

Finally a security door opens to my left. The younger policeman asks me to follow him.

We cross the large room with the glass counter through another door and head for another side door. The officer opens the door and asks me to enter. I am met there by another young slim man in uniform without a jacket. The room is smaller and has wall-to-wall dark wood-fronted cupboards. It just holds the two exaggeratedly large heavy desks, each with a computer screen facing each other.

I notice the dark green rubber writing pads.

The man asks me to sit at the side of one of the desks, with my back to the door. He rolls up the office chair from the other desk.

He sits down at the workstation and turns to me. The seating arrangement seems strangely improvised to me.

I sit and feel out of place.

I try to estimate the age of the young blond policeman. Maybe 28, possibly a little over 30. He is well-groomed, not very tall. I hand him my stack of papers of printed threats, start the conversation with my request and explain how it came about. He lets me finish and looks at me attentively. During my description, I get the impression that he finds me unsympathetic as a person and disapproves of my project. Reluctantly, he begins to skim the pile of printouts. He sorts my printouts by „wishes", as he puts it, and by real threats:

„Get hit by a bus, you deserve to be shot in the head." for example, is the expression of a wish.

„We also invented a nice game: Whoever hits you hard in the face gets € 100. Whoever breaks your bones gets € 200 and whoever beats your fucking brains out gets €700 !

We'll get you, you animal abuser !!!"

written by email by someone who calls himself an animal lover.

That is a criminal offence.

My appearance does not seem to surprise him.

There is a pile of papers on his desk, which he looks through briefly and then turns back to me. The policeman does not manage to hide the fact that he is already aware of my case and that he does not like it.

I try to resume the conversation and explain that I no longer feel safe.

I didn't want to exaggerate because I wasn't in a position to assess how seriously the threats should be taken. In order not to appear embarrassingly over-anxious, I try to put my situation into perspective.

The police officer does not comment further on my description and does not respond to it. Instead, he begins to explain to me in detail the different levels of personal protection.

He also explained that he himself had no influence on the decision whether and when personal protection would be granted. This would have to be applied for and a decision would then be made by a higher authority.

I show understanding, but explain my situation again in more detail. Something seems to be stirring inside him. He pulls out a writing pad and begins to routinely question me about my daily habits. He notes down my answers on his pad. He then pulls a form from a drawer and fills it out by hand. As he enlightens me, he hands me the paper. It is a form for a criminal complaint against unknown persons. He says I can leave it open whether I want to decide within a few weeks whether or not to report the threats of murder and violence.

It seems sensible to me to postpone possible police reports until a later date. I sign, with the thought in mind that the internet should not be a lawless space.[6]

He keeps my printouts and adds them to his pile of other papers. The policeman fails to mention how comprehensively he is informed about my situation at this point by the numerous complaints he has received and by the public prosecutor's office itself. The State Criminal Police Office has started to open a file on me.

The blond policeman turns to me in his chair and looks at me emotionlessly. But then he promises to send the general police patrol past my house at least at night as a protective measure.

At 8.59 p.m. Berthold writes from Dortmund:

„Dear Mr Mehnert,

I congratulate you on your 11 Days project. What a grandiose idea! You can't present it any more vividly than that. PS: Presumably the server will collapse on the deadline ;)"

At 9.03 p.m. Mark L. writes in an email to me:

„Hi dumbass,

I am one of those who heard about your unspeakable action and will be happy if YOU are shot down instead of the rat.

The world has enough terrorists, nobody needs your pseudo-art. You are not only a crazy psychopath, you are also dangerous because you call for violence under the guise of art. Nobody talks about drones in relation to your project. Everyone only talks about the insane animal abuser who is too cowardly to put himself in the box. Let the rat go free and humanity finally have peace. You only contribute to making the world even more aggressive. Otherwise, unfortunately, you are good for nothing. Mark L."

At 11:15 p.m. Mdhater tweets.

@Mdhater

@FlorianMehnert hopefully you're one taken out. Limp dick goof.

Day 7
Tuesday, 17 March

00.16 a.m.
@Mdhater tweets:
@FlorianMehnert someone's going to end your ignorance.

At around 3.20 a.m. I wake up and can't get back to sleep.
I feel the negative force of the shitstorm and the countless
threats crashing down on me.
I am no longer able to suppress the situation any longer.
I get up and wander through the house.
There is unusually bright light outside.
I leave the courtyard and the studio brightly lit all night.
It looks romantic, but the reason for my night lighting, is
fear. I go to my laptop and read more emails.

Someone emails:
„`11 DAYS: Please turn off the lights at least at night!
Fellow species would be good too.
It's torture like this!!!"

Andreas writes:
„Leave it alone! After all, it is a life that you want to ex-
tinguish with your bizarre art project. You have a right to

draw attention to your things … but please not like this. I say this not as an animal rights activist, but as a normal thinking person who still has a kernel of hope…"

A sender with a Russian email address shares:
„I express disrespect to you because your art project is a savagery and the barbarity. It is a pity that the descendant of the great German people is engaged in the similar nonsense, discrediting the idea of art."

And Lisa from Cazadero, CA USA:
„What you are doing is abhorrent. Only monsters that like to kill will respond; do Not give them more of a venue to torture and cause pain than they already have. Stop this project now. Find another way to make your point about drones."

A man from Cologne comments at 5.45 a.m.:
„You want to use killing to draw attention to killing?
What kind of pathological thinking has taken on a life of its own in your insane brain!
You'd better start thinking about whether the internet won't kill you soon!
Let's just hope that there won't be a massacre, you should perish slowly (of course, all in the name of attention!).
You call yourself an artist?
Shall I come and look for you, to let out my creative streak on you?
Any little pisser can lock a rat in a cage and create such a website. Don't imagine that you are something great now.

Because their actions prove the absolute opposite.

It doesn't even matter if it will come to that or not, just the fact that you are pathetic joke, pushing drones to get yourself talked about shows that you are just a miserable pile of shit.

Believe me: I would rather eat that pile of shit than reach out my hand to you!

Why don't you actually squat in a cage?

You are just a pathetic coward with an urge for self-expression, because that's all a scumbag like you is capable of.

Do drones kill rats or people? Who invents this cowardly murder weapon and then uses it?

Shouldn't they use (YES, „use" - to do the same to you -) a human being for it!

For the sake of accuracy, it should be a US-American (agent, mercenary, soldier, politician …), because there such human scum can be found in abundance.

But you are not available for real criticism and active action anyway, you prefer to hide behind so-called „art".

Alternatively, I can offer you to cut off your head to draw attention to the beheadings.

Or you can burn a pregnant 19-year-old alive.

You can also take a 16-year-old or even boys - today one have to say that.

In addition, I would like to draw attention to the so-called Coma kicker, can I count on your head as a target?

I have to kick somewhere, of course all in the guise of artistic creation including livestreams to announce where and how hard I should kick.

GREAT IDEA, isn't it? <-- do I have to reckon with your

lawyer now, you know „Intellectual Property" ….

May you burn in hell, but don't get your hopes up, the rat will most definitely not cross your path there.

I hope that I will be spared from you and your kind in the future. May you suffer an agonizing end, I PLEASE and HOPE so! "

Sidney writes by email

„How dare you?!

MANY PEOPLE HAVE A HEART! AND YOU ARE A SADISTIC MAN WHO HAS NO ARTISTIC SKILLS! KILLING RATS ISN'T A FORM OF ART AT ALL! IF YOU LOVED THE RAT INSTEAD OF KILLING IT, YOU WOULD UNDERSTAND WHY I DON'T SUPPORT YOUR IDEA! I DON'T UNDERSTAND WHY PEOPLE LIKE YOU HAVE TO SHOW THE MONSTER INSIDE! MANY CHOOSE TO HIDE IT! YOU AND ALL THE OTHER SADISTIC PEOPLE IN THIS WORLD SHOULD BE ASHAMED, FUCK YOU AND YOUR „ART" YOU DON'T KNOW WHAT FUCKING ART IS!!!"

Annette K.:

„In a world where children riding bicycles, people walking or dogs in their own garden are shot at, they still support our sick society by taking pleasure in the execution of a rat????

Just sick !!!!

THAT has nothing to do with art, but apparently you have no other way to enter the conversation and the only chance for you is to adapt to our sick society !!!!

Pitiful …..What has become of our beautiful world!?"

Jackie from Australia:

„YOU are a waste of space. Art is not about teaching people to kill. Isn't there enough misery in the world without you adding to it. Get a life."

Dr. B:

11 days - Violation of the Animal Welfare Act

„Dear Mr Mehnert,

the killing of a vertebrate animal for artistic purposes is prohibited. This is a violation of §17 para. 1 TierSchG. Therefore, we from the association [...]would like to ask you emphatically to immediately terminate the project 11 days and to remove it from the homepage. We will also involve the relevant authorities."

Nick from Switzerland:

„Sorry Florian, what kind of perverted A******* are you to do something like this to the rat, you should be put in this cage!"

Angelika E.:

„Dear Mr Mehnert,

I read about your questionable project on the internet. It's just disgusting. Rats are living beings. They feel, sense and think. They are smart and have more sense than some humans. How can you be so perverse?

You disgust me. Plain and simple.

And I wish you all the worst."

A user complains via Twitter because the server has collapsed again.

@Soggsti:
Fuck you @FlorianMehnert : Service Temporarily Unavailable.

Ardilla congratulates:
„Hello,
congratulations on your work .... I think it's very good that this topic is getting into the public eye, because hundreds of outcries for one rat and almost not a single call against the current warfare.
Your project shows a sad reflection of the current social processes. I would like to thank you, even though I question the methodology, as a rat is an animal that should live in society. I would like to offer you to find a suitable place for the rat so that it can find a suitable home after the deadline as opposed to the many victims who actually die by the click of a mouse. Thank you for your provocative work."
I write via Twitter:
#11days, do you accept targeted killing as gamification and the consequence of total surveillance? this #rat can save 1000's of human #lives

@SMdhater
@FlorianMehnert people are going to find you and kill you and we will all rejoice

@She..Speaks..T
@FlorianMehnert @nytimes you're a fucking piece of shit. Get hit by a bus.

via Twitter: @P...
Killing an #animal in the name of Art?!!!
Stop #German #Artist @FlorianMehnert now!!!
thepetitionsite.com/961/709/766/ki...#AnimalPic.Twitter.
com/3VRTpDqpAw

In the end, 11.851 people from many different countries
will have signed this petition via „thepetitionsite.com".
There will be 6 petitions in total with around 35.000 signatories against the project.[7]
People from all over the world will have written me around
500 emails. I cannot quantify the countless comments in
the online newspapers, Facebook, Twitter and other social
networks.

On Tuesday morning, I give an interview to another radio
station. At 11.30 a.m., a television crew from the regional
television station announced that they would be coming.
Around 10.30 a.m., the cast-iron bell on my gate rings.
I react. During my walk to the opaque gate, I see from the
shoes visible underneath that several people are waiting
behind it.
I open the gate and come face to face with three gentlemen in trench coats.
It is not the camera crew.
One of the gentlemen approaches me confidently and au-
thoritatively: „Mr Mehnert?"
I answer in the affirmative.
„We would like to talk to you," he asks in a convincingly
firm voice that brooks no argument.

Caught off guard, I let the three gentlemen enter the courtyard. Silently, I lead the way and then halt hesitantly in front of the front door.

As I turn around, the presumed leader of the trio speaks up again and begins to introduce himself and his companions by name.

The situation slips away from me because at that moment I realise that I am dealing with a superior form of official authority that was previously foreign to me.

The men stand in a semicircle around me and simultaneously pull out their badges, which they routinely hold out to me.

I can't keep up with their pace and only glance at their cards without reading them. When they want to take them again, I insist and ask to see them again. I try to gain time, although I don't know what for.

Mr P., I estimate him to be in his late 50s, is the first to hand me his ID card again.

He is slim and a little taller than me. Over his grey suit he wears an open beige trench coat.

His face, looks narrow, the dark bags under his eyes contrast with his strikingly broad nose. He looks at me with a mockingly smug drawl around the thin corners of his mouth.

He seems to be the talker.

I study his identity card with exaggerated interest, and read there „Senior Government Director/ Head of Department". Abruptly and slightly annoyed, he suddenly snatches his ID from my hand and comments gruffly,

„We're not that pretty on our IDs, Mr Mehnert!"

The other man identifies himself as Detective Chief Inspector Mr G.. He speaks with a slight Swabian accent.

I estimate him to be in his early sixties.

He gives me the experienced impression of an old hand.

His broad round face on his slightly corpulent stocky body smiles at me in a friendly fatherly way.

The third man.

Maybe in his mid-fifties, tall, broad and stocky.

Official veterinarian Dr. vet. K.

I don't remember his name.

Good-naturedly, I follow my cooperative attitude and kindly ask what I can do for the gentlemen.

Head of Department P. briskly takes the floor:

„Can we talk to you in peace, Mr. Mehnert?"

I don't answer and look indecisively through the men into the distance.

The many interviews of the last few days, the short nights, the little sleep, have left me very exhausted.

Irritated, I try to make sense of their sudden appearance.

I suddenly feel powerless and thin-skinned. Several cups of black coffee have catapulted me into the morning.

I adjusted to more scheduled interviews and the camera crew for today.

The thought runs through my mind that I really don't have to tolerate the sudden visit of these three very determined-looking officials.

However, I am unable to translate my thought into consistent action.

The head of the department, P., interrupts me in my viscous indecision:

„We would like to take a look at your installation first, Mr Mehnert!"

"Of course, I'd be happy to," I reply in a run-on manner, trying not to let my uncertainty show.

In the studio, cold air envelops me and I freeze slightly, although the sun shines warmingly outside. I point to the installation, which the three men immediately approach.

Suspiciously humming critical comments, the official veterinarian circles my white rat enclosure illuminated from below. I am pleased by the atmosphere of the laboratory-like sterile lighting.

Meanwhile, the superintendent focuses on the gun and kneels in front of it. I have covered the weapon with yellowish foam.

It is a precaution I have taken because of the journalists.

I want to avoid information about the type of weapon being revealed in a television report.

Chief Superintendent G. asks me to uncover the weapon. He wants to read off an official registration number, which must be stamped somewhere on the weapon.

I comply with his request, loosen some black adhesive tape and carefully peel the weapon out of its foam casing.

The inspector quickly realises that it is a paintball gun. In my opinion, he plays his role excessively seriously. Still kneeling in front of the gun, he asks me to assist him in finding the registration number.

He pretends to be a fatherly swaggerer:

„Mr Mehnert, I don't see so well anymore, could you please help me, there must be a number stamped somewhere on this weapon."

I kneel down close to him and find the number stamped on the side of the trigger.

The inspector asks me to read the number to him.

Patiently, I spell it out while he takes notes on his drawn pad. He straightens up and is unexpectedly vocal:

„Ha, but you're lucky you don't have compressed air connected to the gun and the gun isn't loaded. Then it would be your turn, Mr Mehnert!" and adds:

„Now, I need to see the invoice for the weapon, please."

Then he wants to photograph the registration number and the weapon. I only notice now that he has a camera in his hands.

He is so clumsy when photographing the weapon that he awkwardly bumps into the construction.

I react indignantly, telling him to please be careful, after all, this installation is sensitive and a work of art.

He takes note of my indignation condescendingly shaking his head. Meanwhile, the head of the department, P., striving for authority, creeps around the installation with his hands clasped behind his back.

He stops and turns to me:

„Mr Mehnert, we want to help you."

I don't understand what he means by this and wait for his explanation. „Do you understand me correctly, Mr Mehnert, you have caused quite a stir with your project there and we are primarily concerned with your safety."

I think I can guess what he is getting at.

„However, I have to tell you", his tone becomes more serious, „that we have two positions", he pauses dramatically: „You know, we are for you, but we are also against you."

Grinning meaningfully, he looks at me.

His obviously contrived, contradictory remark annoys me. His face remains contorted into a slightly mocking grin. His eyes narrow, which involuntarily gives him something unserious, smarmy.

The official veterinarian interrupts and asks if he can see the rat. He can't see it, because the rat usually sleeps in its little den during the day.

I then approach the installation, reach in and lift up the little house in which the rat is resting.

The animal is sitting in its nest and is surprised by the disturbance. The rat looks up briefly with its snout, sniffing, before reflexively taking flight.

After a short orientation run, it tries to find shelter in the cardboard tube. I lift up one side of the cardboard tube so that the rat can run out the other side. The veterinarian superfluously comments that the rat is probably in a well-fed, vital condition, although the way it is kept is anything but species-appropriate. I ignore his insinuation.

I silently look at the inside of my installation.

The floor is covered with commercial bedding made of sawdust from the pet shop.

A smell of freshly sawn wood rises from the box.

The rat has spread it irregularly during its exploratory walks, so that the yellowish warm light from below shines well through the milky white of the floor.

The litter is clean. I kept cleaning the enclosure of droppings and food scraps.

I am overcome with a trace of pity for the animal.

Not because of the veterinarian's comment, but because I

am forced to disturb the rat in its sleep and its fearfulness and restlessness comes through to me.

The thought forms in my mind that an unfair game is brewing here.

Three against one.

The chief inspector reports back.

His slight Swabian accent resonates in his pronunciation:
„You know, Mr Mehnert, it's not that we want to accuse you of anything, but we just have to talk to each other."

„We are concerned about your safety, because you have been threatened. You have also asked the police for personal protection."

He plays the role of the fatherly „good cop" quite convincingly.

„As I said, we want to help you,"
echoes the head of the department in the trench coat, now in a friendly voice:

„But you have to cooperate with us."

Resistance begins to stir within me.

The sudden whirring of the moving gun interrupts the conversation.

Silently we watch together the jerking gears of the actuated weapon.

I break through the silence and explain that someone had just logged on from the internet.

Department head P. averts his eyes unimpressed and appraises me. Suddenly he becomes clear unexpectedly quickly:

„Mr Mehnert, we are of the opinion that you should terminate the project promptly for safety reasons. We would also be prepared to take over the rat."

All three men watch me steadfastly.

The constant addressing with my surname annoys me. Also because I couldn't remember the names of the three men so quickly in return and I don't want to give myself the nerve to ask again.

I look around for a suitable answer, but they don't let me get a word in edgewise.

The commissar intervenes:

„Mr Mehnert, you've achieved everything, you've got the attention you wanted, that's enough now."

I defend myself and reply that I have no intention of ending the project and want to elaborate further.

„Mr Mehnert," P. interrupts me irritably, „be reasonable, what else do you want? Don't make trouble now, we want to make it as easy as possible for you. We only want to help you."

I feel like a patient in a psychiatric ward whom doctors want to bring to his senses.

He goes on to say that there are a lot of complaints from the public and they also have an obligation to look after the welfare of the rat.

I pointedly interjected that the rat was doing very well. It has food, fresh water, a shelter and a clean box!

The situation becomes even more tense.

Head of Department P. rises to a new level of sharpness and loud directness: „Mr Mehnert! What do you think is going on here? Our office is inundated with international press enquiries without interruption.

We get calls from the public all the time.

Camera and press teams are camped outside our building! We are busy with nothing more than answering enquiries about your project. My staff complain. This can't go on, do you understand?"

I am amused by his trivial-sounding explanation about alleged complaints from his staff.

I decide to go on to explain further and state frankly that, after all, it was never planned to have the rat killed, but that it was necessary to maintain this as a fiction in the sense of the project's objective. I sense that the head of department is neither convinced of my intention nor of my actual honesty. He does not believe me.

His face reflects mistrust and scepticism.

Obviously, he seems to imply that I want to load the gun at the end of the countdown.

I go on to say that the focus on the rat has admittedly slipped a little. In order to further relativise the situation, I mention that there are thousands of rats in the laboratories of the research and pharmaceutical industries.

Not to mention the countless poisoned rats in the sewers of our cities.

„Yes," the head of department, P., barks sharply at me,

„but you don't see them live on the internet, Mr Mehnert!"

I have to grin.

The head of the department follows up with consistent matter-of-factness:

„We have prepared everything, Mr Mehnert, and would like you to hand over the rat to us now and finish the project. I must point out to you that you are doing this voluntarily, we are not confiscating anything here."

The situation overwhelms me and I try to buy time again.
I make myself hospitable, offer the gentlemen a coffee and refer them to another room outside the studio where they could sit down in peace.

Everyone agrees, but only the head of the department wants a coffee. We step out of the studio and I delegate the men to a ground-level annex with a glassed-in front. I ask the gentlemen to take a seat and go out again. The chief inspector follows me unasked across the courtyard to the kitchen. As we enter the kitchen, he suddenly becomes confidential: „You know, Mr Mehnert, I personally think your project is great. It's great how you're doing it."

I flatter him, but I don't believe his sincerity. I attribute his statement to the „good cop/bad cop" strategy.

„I don't know how you came up with such an idea...

But you know, my opinion can't count here now and I shouldn't really be telling you all this."

I pour coffee into two mugs and look for spoons and sugar. The inspector follows me back to the waiting colleagues.

I have just put the two cups of coffee down on a low table near the uninvited guests when the announced camera team appears.

It is the reporter Markus H., accompanied by another reporter I don't know from Stuttgart, a cameraman and a sound man. I know Markus from earlier TV reports he shot about my work.

The TV crew is standing in the warm bright sun in the middle of the courtyard. I walk towards them dejectedly, greet Markus and the others friendly, the chief inspector at my back again.

When the commissioner spots the crammed cameraman with TV camera on his shoulder, he holds his open hand in front of the camera and shouts,

„No pictures please!"

and then, turning to me, grins,

„You know, I'm TV-shy by profession, right."

I am just about to explain the situation, when Commissioner P. comes shooting from behind. Quickly, his coat billowing, he jumps towards the camera team and raises his hands defensively as he begins to speak:

„Stop, we can't have television here now!"

Rigorously he explains that they don't want a camera here now and that they have to talk to Mr Mehnert for a while longer.

Without any further explanation of his person, he plays out his authority and makes it unmistakably clear to the camera team that they must leave immediately.

With a gesture of helplessness, I meet Markus' questioning gaze.

„Can you come back later?", I hear myself say.

Visibly surprised at the situation, but also interested because he senses an exciting story:

„Yeah sure, no problem, we'll stay around here and come back later, you can always reach me on the mobile".

The cameraman and the sound man remain standing in the courtyard for a few moments, still undecided, when Markus asks them to leave with a wave of his hand.

I walk with the two men back into the room overlooking the inner courtyard, which is furnished in a reduced way with a small white sofa and two armchairs facing each other. Before I turn to the men, I watch the camera team disappear through the gate.

Chief Superintendent G. and Department Head P. take a seat in the armchairs, the veterinarian is standing in the background. I do not offer him a seat and sit down alone on the sofa. The head of the department takes up the floor again and explains conciliatorily:

„Excuse me, but we really don't need television here now, surely you understand?"

He has put on his slightly mocking thin smile again.

I sip my sweet black coffee and try powerlessly to sort out my thoughts.

I think of the sleepless night's conversation with Brad about ending it prematurely.

The project has reached its zenith. That's for sure.

It could, on the other hand, get more attention, of course. There are still many open requests from other TV stations and radio stations.

New ones are coming in all the time.

I remember that later at 2 p.m. I have arranged an interview with the state broadcaster of Swedish radio. Then at 2.30 p.m. with a radio station from Bremen.

I notice how burnt out I am by the marathon of the many press enquiries.

The pressure of the shitstorm has manifested itself in me as a psychological burden that I try in vain to suppress.

I feel a chill.

My thoughts are interrupted by the ringing of the telephone. It's a high-spirited reporter from a private radio station in Vienna.

She wants an interview for a television report.

I put her off and ask her to send me her contact details by e-mail.

The broadcast will take place later without me.

In an obvious hurry, an expert from a well-known art auction house is invited instead, who is asked the next morning in conversation with two presenters whether my installation is art at all.

The head of department, P., gets through to me from his armchair:

„Mr Mehnert, we propose the following deal:

You hand over the rat to us now and we will then issue a press release stating that we have taken custody of the rat and that it was kept in a species-appropriate manner and with care. We will announce that the rat is safe."

„You do want all this protest from the animal rights activists to finally stop. You know, we are quite concerned for your safety."

The inspector interferes and adds in his fatherly Swabian way:

„Mr Mehnert, you have applied for personal protection, you are entitled to that, but I have to process your case and help decide in what form we can arrange protection for you. But that presupposes that you also cooperate. You cannot simply expose yourself to a self-generated threat and then not cooperate. Just think of your family!"

I don't feel like responding to his words.

It's all happening too fast for me.

I straighten up and inform him that I am not interested in the press statement of the district administration.

After all, I have enough press of my own in which I can explain in detail what is important to me.

Department head P., in his trench coat, which he has not taken off all this time, jerks up from his chair. He takes a few angry quick steps across the room, collects himself and turns to me. His voice becomes emphatically calm, but strikes a threatening undertone.

He speaks his words stressedly slowly as he walks back towards me:

„You see, Mr Mehnert, I always try to do good first.

That is my way. I am a fair partner.

I am always willing to talk to the people concerned first.

I am not the type of person who immediately threatens with the paragraphs and with punishment."

He sits back in the chair, opens his knees and leans far forward towards me with his elbows up.

As he focuses on my face, he cannot suppress his thin grin:

„But I want to tell you one thing, Mr Mehnert:

we don't have anything concrete against you yet, we can't force you to end the project here and now, but ...",

he pauses dramatically and takes a breath. His smile dies as his eyes search for contact with me.

Serenely, the words leave his mouth:

„If you are not willing to cooperate, Mr Mehnert, then we will find something against you. I can assure you of that!"

Silence grips the room.

I realise his words as a sudden threat.

A wave of indecision spreads through me. My thoughts begin to rotate, I am flooded with fantasies: I see myself skidding in my car with defective brakes. They discover drugs in my boot during a traffic check.

I wipe the carousel of thoughts aside inwardly, try to block out the plainclothes officers in the room and get a clear thought. My thoughts now circle around the shape of a possible ending.

The thought of ending the project relieves me.

I want to find the right time to end the experiment.

When is the right time?

Since the nightly chat with Brad, it is clear to me that I will not let the eleven-day countdown come to an end. There is no doubt that the response to my project `11 DAYS´ has been unexpectedly great. The project has generated worldwide excitement. People are discussing it.

In all kinds of forums and in the social media.

Has `11 DAYS´ achieved its goal?

I don't want to overstep the mark.

Are the officials beating me to it now? Or am I not already at the point of ending the project anyway?

I continue to think.

Later, the camera crew will come back. I could convince them to continue to accompany me throughout the day. They could report an early end. What will happen if I just send the officials away now? Will I need more time?

Won't they come back anyway?

Does a refusal make sense? Will it help my project in terms of content if I continue now?

How will the `11 DAYS´ reverberate if I continue with the project?

A feeling of fear, vague and not definable:

I fear escalation.

Another long overdue consideration pushes itself to the fore: who actually sent these men?

Does their appearance possibly originate from a higher authority? Did the three men actually come on their own initiative? Is the head of the department joining forces with a chief detective and a veterinary officer on his own initiative to set off together? Just to convince an artist who has become annoying to stop his art project?

Who has so much interest in a premature end?

I doubt the initiative of the three men in plain clothes.

I will never get answers to my questions.

A large number of criminal complaints will have been received from private individuals, but also from lawyers, and my file at the public prosecutor's office will grow to three hundred and eighty pages.

In the information I later request from the State Criminal Police Office, it is confirmed that I am on file there because of my project.

The art experiment `11 DAYS´ has reached its climax.

I decide to end the project on Tuesday 17 March at 7 p.m.

„But not that you'll put in a second new rat again and continue the project after we've gone!" leader P. comments pointedly on my loudly expressed decision.

I almost feel insulted at the obviously deep mistrust and at the same time ashamed of my good-natured naivety. Suddenly a French proverb from my school days comes to mind in relation to Dezernent P.:

„Honi y soit qui mal y pense".[8]

I assure him that I am determined to finish the project today and hand the rat over to the authorities. Department head P. jumps up triumphantly and becomes impatient. He has not touched his coffee.

The veterinarian hastily leaves the room to return with a cage, which he has obviously already deposited in the car as a precaution. I ask for the telephone number of the department's press officer, because I want to arrange with him the time of publication of his statement. The men accompany me back to my studio and approach the installation, confident of victory. The official veterinarian tries to lift the rat out of the box. As if the rat suspects what is about to happen, it resists loudly. It squeals, wriggles and bites the veterinarian's hand.

Dejectedly, I watch the scenario unfold. My thoughts turn to the organisational work that now lies ahead of me. The vet then gets hold of the rat. With further squirming and wriggling, he resolutely transports it into the container he has brought with him.

In the nine-page statement of the public prosecutor's office on the application of artistic freedom in relation to the art experiment `11 DAYS´, I will later read that the voluntary handing over of the rat to the authorities would have supported the credibility of my claim that I had not intended to allow the rat to be shot.

The gentlemen ask to leave my studio through the back door. They want to escape the camera crew that might be lying in wait. Resignedly, I unlock the back door of my studio for them.

Chief Inspector B. pauses briefly to hand me his business card and ask me to send him the e-mails with the threats of violence and murder.

He promises to take care of it.

I will not hear from him again.

I later filed a criminal complaint against all the threats myself. In a later order of the public prosecutor's office I read:

„Due to a killing of a rat presented by the complainant as a provocative art action on the internet, on a certain day by remote triggering of a firearm aimed at it, a large number of criminal complaints [...] were received by the authorities involved [...].

At the same time, however, the injured party also received a large number of emails in which he himself was threatened with crime and insulted.

The examination of these emails did not provide any starting points for an investigation of the perpetrators. As a rule, the true user cannot be identified from e-mail addresses, as was the case here. Email addresses are always registered via the Internet and from a home PC. Especially in cases like the present one, where crimes are committed or threatened, registration is done under alias data in order not to enable criminal prosecution. The intention to conceal is already recognisable from the names of the senders used. The proceedings therefore had to be discontinued for factual reasons."

The camera team will be back any moment.

I suppress a pang of disappointment and anger at myself. I feel exhausted.

The end brought about by myself is too sudden for me. On the other hand, relieving. I still have a lot to prepare for tonight's announcement. There is not much time left.

David B. Writes from a google email address:

„What a fucking whore you are!

turn off the fucking webcam, you fucking animal quitter!

HOW ABOUT HAVING A GUN TO YOUR HEAD ??"

A man with an email address on AOL writes:

„What goes around comes around, let's see how long you can dodge your bullit.

Your gonna need eyes in the back of your head if you carry out your immature stunt I'll be coming for you"

Alex H. from Belgium with Outlook address writes:

„You filthy bitch, you deserve to die! It's inhumane, dirty, barbaric, disgusting what you're trying to do.... You are a poor shit, I wish the same thing to happen to you, and that you squirm under the greatest suffering in existence, that you be left to die in your own shit in a prison cell without drink and food and sleep. If you hurt this poor little rat you will pay dearly, there are millions out there mobilising to protect her!"

Calls to join petitions against `11 DAYS´ are being retweeted on Twitter.

When I step out of the studio, Markus and his team are already standing in the courtyard. They must have watched the three men drive away.

I tell them about my decision.

The television crew is surprised and at first perplexed, disappointed. I catch their perplexity and we all sit down together in the sun with another coffee and discuss the course of the remaining afternoon and evening.

The camera team agrees to stay until the end and accompany me through the rest of the day until evening.

Again and again the phone rings with press enquiries.

I write a circular email to the press announcing the end of the project this evening at 7 p.m..

As planned, I will hang photos of drone victims in the box of the installation. I haven't had time to prepare them yet, so I start by cutting up the photos I already have ready and then laminate them onto cardboard.

The camera team films me and asks questions.

After all the discussions about the rat, my intention is to bring the focus clearly back to the issue of armed drones.

In between, I give the planned interview with Swedish radio. The two young people from Sweden greet me cheerfully, openly and casually through the phone.

„Hi Florian, how are you?"

I answer their superficial questions in a friendly manner and then start talking myself into a rage.

In a monologue, I excitedly explain my intention, the reactions of the recipients and my interpretation of it. I name Germany's involvement in the drone wars. I talk about the recipients' excessive demands, about the stupidity of some, about the death threats. It bubbles up, it all bursts out of me. I get the feeling that the two young Swedes must have planned a hip, cool interview. They didn't expect the sudden unfiltered emotional eruption of my serious flow of words. At the other end of the phone line it is getting quieter and quieter. They don't seem to want to ask their probably prepared questions anymore.

I have destroyed their concept.

I feel how startled they are at me, at what I am explaining and elaborating to them.

In a hoarse voice I continue: „Do we all want to accept targeted killing on suspicion by remote-controlled drones? Do we even live in a constitutional system? Do we want to accept that people are killed without a hearing, without a trial, virtually over the internet? Not to mention the civilian victims who were in the vicinity of the alleged victim."

My directness overwhelms them.

I get the impression that only now, while talking to me on the phone, are they beginning to understand my project.

I keep talking and forget my time pressure about it.

The television crew is waiting patiently outside.

I blurt out:

„I have applied for police protection. There are countless charges against me, the shitstorm never stops. There are moronic people out there who shift the focus to saving the rat and who would rather kill the artist instead.

The public prosecutor's office is investigating.

Just now three civilian officers were here and, without a criminal offence, forced the end of my project.

I handed over the rat to the officers earlier.

But the project has reached its zenith!

The project ends at 7 p.m. today."

I don't know if this interview was ever broadcast on Swedish radio.

By the time Brad gets up at 7.45 a.m. in Texas, I have already briefed him via the Google Hangout:

„Brad, the rat is out of the box. I've turned it over to the authorities. I'm going to finish the project today. I'll talk to you later …"

When he asks why and I briefly describe the morning's proceedings, he only comments:

„Wow… the rat doesn't even know how important it is!"

By email I arrange another interview with English radio in the evening at 10 p.m.

In a blog entry I read:

„I feel that there is a lot to learn from these works…

After signing the Vargas petition back in 2008, I am now both proud and regret it. The point of artworks like this is for us to transgress the bigger idea that enable us to better ourselves as human beings. Make us think of the anonymous killers and the unnecessary suffering in the world. The rat is an innocent, humanity has a choice: destroy or save, just like our choices we make every day. Any act of protest will contribute to the work.

We are the work.

The petition is the work, me typing this is the work, as I am contributing live thoughts about Florian Mehnert, and it is terrifyingly beautiful.

I hope that the internet do not shoot the Rat, although we shall see what the cruelty of humanity can do when the killer is anonymous and no blame shall be put on the person. There is no authority telling us, just merely saying that we could.

While the days pass when the work is active, THINK, and before you sign any petition, do the research, look for the reasoning behind the existence of the work from a non subjective viewpoint, you might be pleasantly surprised. [...]"

In place of the countdown, the words: GAME OVER
Now appearing in red.

On the website I publish the text:
„The art experiment `11 DAYS´ has successfully reached its goal and ended on 17 March 2015 at 19:00 (CET). The rat is alive and has left the installation.
It was never intended for the artistic statement of the experiment to actually open up the possibility of shooting the lab rat."

After the premature countdown ends, positive feedback comes in via email.
The audience seems to lean back and relax.

Day 8
Wednesday, 18 March

In the morning, the singer of an experimental Viennese pop duo sends an email with a link to her private soundcloud account. She congratulates me on my project. The first song is called „Lab rats, escape!"

Throughout the day I continue to give interviews about the end of the project. Many newspapers and radio stations now want to talk to me again.

At 10 a.m., a video journalist from a large national newspaper visits me. I have arranged one of my last telephone interviews with another journalist at 2 p.m. It will be for a radio magazine for media and digital culture.[9]

The journalist calls punctually at 2 p.m.

He is in New York and listens to me patiently.

It is a very quiet conversation lasting over an hour, in which I find a chance for the first time after all the countless interviews of the past days to calmly try to reflect on my project:

„Every comment on ˋ11 DAYSˊ, whether positive, restrained, or negative, is a reaction and reflects its impact. ˋ11 DAYSˊ has moved people's thoughts and emotions. Caused them to applaud it, reject it or hate it. At its peak, the art experiment ˋ11 DAYSˊ engaged hundreds of thousands of people worldwide. My intention was to offer a platform of discourse. To open an emotional access about the subject of drone operations and their backgrounds. There are no right or wrong results with regard to the art experiment `11 DAYS´. All reactions to it were right."

At the end, I ask the rhetorical question in the interview: „Wasn't the audience itself the rat in this experiment?"

In the evening, Sebastian M. writes in an email:

„Good evening Mr Mehnert,

Today I heard your statement on the „Eleven Days Project" on DLF [Deutschlandfunk] during tractor work in the vines (I am a vintner).

Against the background of the US drone mania, I find the idea for this „production" ingenious.

The reactions are frightening and reflect a worrying development in our society.

It's great that there are people like you who use creative means to put their finger on the problem.

You have my respect and thanks!

Epilogue

The Role of the Rat

The laboratory rat takes its place as an established laboratory animal in research and teaching. I wanted to give my art experiment a scientific component. Choosing a rat for this seemed contextually appropriate. A mouse (which the rat was mistaken for from time to time in the media) was too small for my purposes because of its size. A mouse would have been more difficult to perceive in the live stream.

The rat's relationship to humans is subject to a certain ambivalence. On the one hand, there is the researched intelligence of the rat, also in its social behaviour, on the other hand, the rat is rather negatively anchored in the collective consciousness as a plague and carrier of epidemics in our culture. It is kept as a popular pet, but then sold as live snake food in pet shops. Even my „lab rat", which was not a lab rat but came from the pet shop, would undoubtedly have died within a few days in the maw of a snake. I deliberately called the rat a lab rat and did not give it a name.

It was meant to be a reference to the well-known use of the rat in experiments in science. And also a hint that my project was an experiment.

The rat played the role of the innocent victim. It stood as a placeholder for the human being. The rat was the calculated trigger for emotions and attention. I hoped that an innocent rat being publicly threatened with a gun would provoke outrage and a sense of injustice.

This is of course where the public announcement of the execution and the portrayal via the livestream plays an important role.

Someone who puts out rat poison in his cellar because his supplies are constantly being eaten and posts or tweets this on Facebook will probably not immediately expose himself to an international shitstorm. Here, the rat must at least accept the reproach of being a pest. In this respect, its punishment by poisoning is more likely to be accepted.

Many of the recipients suggested that I should put myself in the box instead of the rat, that would be art.

This „variant" was excluded for me from the outset in the conception of the project. In my art experiment, I wanted to shift the focus from humans to a placeholder. I didn't want to directly threaten a human being, as is the case with the armed drones, but rather a parallel shift to an abstracted model situation.

It was precisely the credible threat of the rat that made people sit up and take notice, not the much more implausible threat of a human being.

I doubt that the recipients would have been equally outraged by the rescue of the innocent artist from the installation.

The abstraction opens up a new unencumbered access to the subject of drone warfare for the recipient.

The emotionalisation and outrage has clearly succeeded with the rat. I am often asked about the whereabouts of the rat. In a police report, which I am able to see later, there is talk of it being taken to an animal shelter.

The Focus on the Rat

The art experiment `11 DAYS´ showed the doomed rat via livestream. The helplessness of the cute rat generated outrage. The barrel of the controllable weapon was always visible in the picture. The possibility that the rat would be killed at the end of the 11-day countdown was an inescapable fact for many of the recipients. In their perception, these recipients anticipated a definite end to the project: the rat will be killed. However, as can be seen in some online comments, other recipients were aware that I would not risk the rat's life.

In terms of my intention, it would not have made sense in terms of content. In the ‚Forest Protocols‘ and also in the installation ‚Human Tracks‘ I used surveillance to draw attention to surveillance.

In `11 DAYS´, too, the surveillance of the rat through the livestream was significant. Beyond that, however, I wanted to point out the consequence of killing by remote-controlled armed drones as a result and effect of surveillance. I did not intend to draw attention to killing through real killing. For death or killing as the irrevocable end of life transports in its irreversibility a dimension of a completely different scope. Of course, I cannot find any justification in killing for whatever artistic argument. Therefore, the fiction of the rat's possible death was perfectly sufficient for my artistic intention. A supposed fact, disseminated through the media, develops a resounding effect. In its tightrope walk along reality, fiction develops its own powerful dynamic.

It then seems almost impossible for the recipient to distinguish at which point reality turns into fiction. In `11 DAYS´ I even go so far as to put fiction on the same level as reality. Today I would call this approach „live deepfake".

For the recipients, `11 DAYS´ only existed on the internet. No one could visit the installation in reality.

But `11 DAYS´was not a virtual computer game.

The installation was real, the rat inside was real, the execution would have been possible. The website with its livestream represented the transmission medium of the real and interactive installation. Only the actual opening of the possibility of a killing was fiction. In view of this, it is not surprising that many of the recipients recognised the fiction of the planned execution of the rat as reality. The functionality was clearly underpinned by the weapon controllable via computer or smartphone. The planned death of the rat became an unverifiable reality. However, my statements in the many interviews created deliberate doubts in the listener. Again and again during the project I tried to adjust the focus away from the rat to the actual intention of the project. However, the idea of the rat's possible death was obviously more impressive for many. The anticipation of the dead rat seemed to override my intention in many cases.

Why did many people not want to see the clearly formulated intention behind `11 DAYS´?

The art project`11 DAYS´ demanded from its audience the ability to abstract. `11 DAYS´ expected a transfer performance. In the rat that is threatened via the internet, the audience was supposed to see the placeholder for the human being that is threatened by armed drones. Some people may have been overwhelmed with this requirement, or refused to fulfil the transfer performance. The livestream and sight of the rat being threatened over the internet made such an impression that for many, no abstraction was possible. Instead of taking the installation as an occasion to reflect on the use of armed drones, it seemed more worthwhile to save the rat. Paradoxically, some people even suggested my death, the killing of the artist. The audience's behaviour possibly arose from a reaction in terms of their self-efficacy: saving the rat seemed possible and feasible. Influencing the complex processes behind the deployment of armed drones as comparatively impossible and futile. `11 DAYS` did not want to provide answers or solutions. The art experiment raised critical questions and wanted to initiate thought processes.

The Shitstorm

The `11 DAYS´ shitstorm was much more than an expression of disparagement of my person.

The shitstorm was an expression of the recipients' excessive demands and helplessness. It was at the same time an emotional reaction valve, but also experimental proof of massive emotional contagion through social networks. I also refer here to research results by Adam Kramer.[10]

Kramer showed in three studies on Facebook that emotional states can be transmitted to others via social networks. He provided experimental evidence that emotional contagion occurs over online networks without direct interaction, in the complete absence of non-verbal signals and cues between people. Exposure to a friend expressing an emotion is sufficient.

With great speed within a few hours, information about `11 DAYS´ spread.

With equally great speed, emotions boiled up in the networks. With many posts it is questionable whether the short text on the website or the many other background information about `11 DAYS´ were ever read or heard. It seemed to be about following the swarm and sharing the great horror.

The supposed anonymity on the internet did not superficially play a very big role in this. Many of the recipients gave their full name, only a few used an anonymous e-mail address or a nickname. Perhaps the openness of the aggression or the threats can be explained by the medium of the internet, which removed reality through interactivity and livestreaming. Sitting in a kitchen, office or café and being part of a reality that is taking place somewhere broadcast over the internet still seems to create an alienation.

Watching a situation live via the internet and even being able to control it is different from being physically present. If one looks at the hate speech that is held on Facebook, Reddit, Twitter, Telegram and other platforms, one can interpret this as a similar principle of behaviour. The shitstorm on the art experiment `11 DAYS´ can also be seen as a reaction of emotional or mental overload in dealing with a complex reality that is obviously becoming more difficult to penetrate and cope with.

The internet delivers a flood of information every day, often in real time. Coping with all this information is almost impossible and suggests an increasingly complex world. Events in the world's societies are probably no more complex or numerous than they were in the pre-Internet era, it's just that we now have access to all this information simultaneously. The sheer volume of information seems impenetrable, the reality seems more complex. Rescuing or working to save a rat, on the other hand (e.g. in the form of the numerous petitions), seems to transform helplessness into meaningful action. The signatories of petitions to save a single rat unconsciously express: „I have no chance against decisions of a state, what can I do about it. But against the installation of an artist, against a private person, there I can sign, here I can have an effect and thus express my rage about injustice. The helplessness of not being able to effectively campaign against the drone war therefore manifested itself for the „shitstormers" possibly all the more in a rescue of the rat, and in a condemnation of the art project as well as its creator.

At this point, I would like to bring attention to the fact that a shitstorm is not necessarily a reflection of a social reality on the Internet. Looking at the user statistics I have, about 35% of the recipients who participate in the shitstorm are in the minority, while 65% make no statement or a positive statement. It becomes clear from this simple fact that a smaller group via social media is capable of achieving a great media impact with a moral statement and is thus able to influence public opinion in the long term.

This danger has been thoroughly investigated and recognised a few years after my project by, among others, the Brexit campaign in England and the Trump presidential election in the USA, both of which made extensive use of Facebook and Twitter.

Annotations

1 Süddeutsche Zeitung, Radikales Kunstexperiment als Protest gegen Drohnen - 13. März 2015, http://www.sueddeutsche. de/digital/interaktive-kunst-ich-rech- ne-mit-einem-massa-ker-1.2390433

This list of reporting is not complete and represents only a selection:

2 Der Spiegel, Künstler lässt auf Ratte schießen „Ich muss Grenzen überschreiten", 13.03.2015, https://www.spiegel.de/ kultur/gesellschaft/kuenstler-flori- an-mehnert-laesst-publi-kum-auf-ratte-schiessen-a-1023396.html
• The Mirror, UK, Web users given power to kill a rat with their phones as part of an ‚art project'
http://www.mirror.co.uk/news/weird-news/web-users-given-po-wer-kill-5341723,
• Der Standard, Österreich, Kunstaktion zu Drohnen und Überwachung: Internetuser dürfen Ratte töten, 14. März 2015, http://derstandard.at/2000012931606/Kunstaktion-zu-Droh-nen-und-Ueberwachung-Internetuser-duerfen-Ratte-toeten
• DIE WELT, KULTUR, EGO-SHOOTING, Das Internet wird diese Ratte töten, 14.03.15 ,
http://www.welt.de/kultur/kunst-und-architektur/artic-le138416884/Das-Internet-wird-diese-Ratte-toeten.html
• Deutschlandradio Kultur, AKTION GEGEN DROHNENKRIEG, Florian Mehnert im Gespräch mit Stephan Karkowsky, http:// www.deutschlandradiokultur.de/aktion-gegen-droh-nen- krieg-die-ratte-darf-leben-der.2156.de.html?dram:article_

id=314600"

• Stern, Krasses Kunstprojekt Jeder darf diese Ratte erschießen, 14.03.2015, https://www.stern.de/panorama/jeder-darf-diese-ratte-erschiessen--florian-mehnert-schockiert-mit-kunstprojekt--11-tage--5919376.html

• SWR2, Journal am Mittag, Der Aktionskünstler Florian Mehnert und sein Kunstexperiment, 18.3.2015 ,

• DIE WELT, Kunstexperiment,
Darf man eine Ratte per Mausklick töten?, 18/03/2015 , http://www.welt.de/138563631

• SWR Fernsehen, umstrittene Kunstaktion 11 Tage, http://www.swr.de/landesschau-aktuell/bw/umstrittene-kunst- aktion-11-tage-projekt-beendet-ratte-gerettet/-/id=1622/ did=15236848/ nid=1622/1hz933a/

• The Times, UK, One mouse click and a rat dies in artist's protest against drones , http://www.thetimes.co.uk/tto/news/world/europe/artic- le4381300.ece

• Süddeutsche Zeitung, Umstrittenes Experiment beendet
„Ich lasse doch keine Ratte abknallen", 19. März 2015 , http://www.sueddeutsche.de/kultur/umstrittenes-experi- ment-beendet-ich-lasse-doch-keine-ratte-abknallen-1.2399180

• NOS, Netherland, De Duitser en zijn rat: zou jij schieten? , http://nos.nl/op3/artikel/2024844-de-duitser-en-zijn-rat-zou-jij-schieten.html

• France 3, Rat visé par une arme à feu : un artiste allemand abandonne son installation, 18/03/2015 , http://france3-regions.francetvinfo.fr/alsace/2015/03/18/rat-vi- se-par-une-arme-feu-un-artiste-allemand-abandonne-son-in- stallation-677559.html

• Badische Zeitung, Mehnerts Aktion sorgt für Empörung, 17. März 2015, http://www.badische-zeitung.de/.../mehnerts-aktion-sorgt-fuer-empoerung-- 101926798.html,

• SRF, Schweizer Radio und Fernsehen, Ratte im Focus - das um- strittene Kunstprojekt von Florian Mehnert, Kultur Kompakt, 17.03.2015 , http://www.srf.ch/sendungen/kultur-kom-pakt/ratte-im-fo- kus-das-umstrittene-kunstprojekt-von-flori-an-mehnert",

• NDR.de - Kultur, Rattenexperiment gegen totale Überwachung, Florian Mehnert im Interview http://www.ndr.de/kultur/ Meh- nert-im-Interview,mehnert104.html,

• The Mirror, UK, Web users given power to kill a rat with their phones as part of an ,art project' http://www.mirror.co.uk/news/ weird-news/web-users-given-po - wer-kill-5341723,

• Badische Zeitung, Differenzierung findet nicht statt" BZ-INTERVIEW Florian Mehnert http://www.badische-zeitung.de/.../ differenzierung-fin- det-nicht-statt--101865429

• Deutschlandfunk Corso, Kunst - Netz-Installation „11 Tage", Florian Mehnert im Gespräch mit Susanne Luerweg , html,http://www.deutschlandfunk.de/kunst-netz-installati-on-11-tage-abgebrochen.807.de.html?dram:article_id=314724

• Badische Zeitung, Welche Botschaften das Rattenexperiment hat, 19. März 2015 , http://www.badische-zeitung.de/.../wel-che-botschaften-das-rattenexperiment-hat--102049546.html

3 https://www.theguardian.com/news/2019/nov/18/killer-dro-nes-how-many-uav-predator-reaper

4 https://www.florianmehnert.de/waldprotokolle.html

5 http://www.menschentracks.florianmehnert.de/

6 I later requested a reopening of the case with jusristian support, which dragged on for years. Some of the threateners were located.

7 Chance.org, https://www.change.org/p/florian-mehnert-stop-pen-sie-das-rattenexperiment
• thepetitionsite.com, https://www.thepetitionsite.com/de/961/709/766/ki%E2%80%A6/
• Keine Ausstellungen für Tierquäler! https://www.change.org/p/mak-frankfurt-a-m-essenheimer-kunstverein-markgr%C3%A4f-ler-museum-kunsthaus-l6-keine-ausstellungen-f%C3%BCr-tier-qu%C3%A4ler
• Stoppen Sie das Rattenexperiment von Florian Mehnert!, https://www.change.org/p/veterin%C3%A4ramt-m%C3%BCll heim-m%C3%BCllheimer-b%C3%BCrgermeisterin-astrid-sie-mes-knoblich-tierschutzbeauftragte-baden-w%C3%BCrttem-berg-dr-cornelie-j%C3%A4ger-stoppen-sie-das-rattenexperi-ment-von-florian-mehnert

8 „A scoundrel who thinks evil of it", or „Shame on him who thinks evil of it". The phrase is used ironically in French to indicate or imply hidden immoral motives in apparently unsuspicious or morally presented actions.

9 Deutschlandfunk Kultur, WIE DAS KUNSTPROJEKT „11 TAGE" FÜR FURORE SORGTE, Thomas Reintjes hat darüber mit dem Künstler gesprochen, 21.03.2015
https://www.deutschlandfunkkultur.de/netzkultur-vorzeitig-be-endet-100.html

10 Experimental evidence of massive-scale emotional contagion through social networks

Adam D. I. Kramer, Jamie E. Guillory, and Jeffrey T. Hancock

PNAS June 17, 2014 111 (24) 8788-8790; published ahead of print June 2, 2014, https://doi.org/10.1073/pnas.1320040111